I0531054

Dirty Red: A Killa's Love Story

Dirty Red: A Killa's Love Story

Dedications/Acknowledgments

For my dear sister Moon. Your foresight, dedication, and execution are nothing short of awe inspiring

Dirty Red
A Killa's Love Story

MIG

Dirty Red: A Killa's Love Story

Central Park, NYC

"Aye yo, get yo dirty ass up outta here nigga! We got a couple of VIPs coming through," this from a young man in a razor sharp, black suit. Armani, which was expensive attire for a hired goon. He nudged the homeless man lying in the grass with a polished loafer, wet with dew. The homeless man shrugged and mumbled something neither the thug nor his partner, another well-dressed hired gun, could make out.

"Come on mane, get yo shitty ass up outta here before we Abner Louima yo ass," his partner chimed in. He passed on giving a warning nudge with his foot and went straight for a kick to the man's abdomen. The homeless man, who wore a tattered, shit-grey pair of dungarees, a stained, ripped t-shirt, and an army-issued plastic rain cloak, recoiled and moaned in pain. Both men laughed and continued to talk shit when laughter of a different sort cut theirs short.

A laughing little boy - a toddler - an Emanuel Lewis look-alike had he been a few inches taller, chased a red soccer ball several feet behind them.

3

Mig

Walking with a steady stride behind the boy was a hulk of a man - six foot six, weighing nearly three hundred pounds. His jet black, bald head glistened with sweat under the afternoon sun. Although it was faint, the scent of death on him was evident. Annoyed at the commotion, he glanced at his two bodyguards and then back to his son where his frown became something closer to a smile, but not quite.

"Shit! It's Big Ross," the first man cursed under his breath. "Yo, raise the fuck up nigga!" He whispered harshly. "My boss don't like no broke niggas around when he spending time with his...!" Suddenly, the homeless man jumped up and was in the man's face slashing upwards with his hand, then just as quickly dropped low, sweeping him off his feet. As the guard fell, the homeless man continued waving his hands over him in a quick, moving pattern. As he went down, the hoodlum caught a glimpse of metal in the man's hands. He could feel thin slices opening up all around his neck, face, and shoulder region. It was that stinging burn you feel when you've accidentally sliced yourself with a knife while cutting a lemon, but multiplied in length and depth.

Dirty Red: A Killa's Love Story

As his partner hit the ground in a spray of blood, the other guard released a slight scream and stumbled backwards while fumbling for his gun. The surprise attack caught him slipping and he had no time to recover. The homeless man skillfully forced the feather light straight edge he held into the man's mouth, pushing it far back into his skull, like force-feeding cake to the birthday boy who refused to blow out his candles.

"What the fuck!" Big Ross yelled and reached for the clip at his waist. Like a cat playing with a ball of yarn, the homeless man dropped to the grass, rolled to the side, a slate grey Walther PPK 7.65 mm in his hand. He let off a single shot that found its way right between Ross's eyes. The man's white pupils quickly turned plum red with blood. The boy screamed as his father went down, clutching a black 9mm in hand.
The boy growled at the homeless man the way children do when they realize they're not getting desert for not finishing dinner. Swiftly, the youngster ripped the nine millimeter from his father's death grip and took aim.

The homeless man warned, "Don't do it!" Unfortunately, the boy never had a chance. The man's natural reflexes had already taken over.

Mig

He released another shot that found its mark between the youngster's eyes, exploding his brain from the back of his head in a shower of blood and meaty pulp. The homeless man gave two quick glances behind him, and then quickly walked over to the dead bodies, snapping several pictures with his iPhone.

"Youngest one yet," he muttered gravely while staring into the dead boy's blood red eyes. "Shit. Couldn't be helped. Job complete."

Killa Cartel 1

Chapter 1: NYC Health & Racquet Club, 76th St.

"Thank you Tom and good afternoon. This is Ayuki Tomogawa and I'm with city Detective, Lance Brahca coming to you live from the scene of a gruesome crime committed just off the Big Lawn in Manhattan's Central Park." The lean Asian woman was model esque, and wore a slim navy blazer and matching pencil skirt the Detective found pleasing. "Detective, according to your NYPD colleagues, four people have been gunned down, including a six or seven-year-old boy. Any idea of the identities of the victims and or perpetrator?"

"I'm sorry Ayuki; I don't have those answers for you at the moment. As a matter of fact, I'm going to need you and your people to clear the area please," Detective Brahca, a youngish Magnum P.I., without the mustache or tan leathery skin, kept his eyes glued to her chest as he spoke.

"We've spoken to an officer who agreed to speak under the condition of anonymity as he's not authorized to comment on the case," continued the reporter unperturbed.

"He told us he believes the victims to be Ross Mitgowen, aka Big Ross, one of New York City's most notorious street pharmacists, his young son, and two armed men whom they believe served as Mitgowen's bodyguards."

"As I said before dear, as soon as we ascertain all the facts, you'll be the first to know. Until then, get the hell off of my crime scene," ordered Detective Brahca as he waved her away.

"I find your attitude highly condescending detective. A child has been killed," snapped the reporter, disappointed.

"Professionalism! Whatever happened to it?" Asked Black Pops, tapping his cigar into a crystal mosaic ashtray. Dressed all in black, loafers, slacks, sports coat, and turtleneck, he sat in a cushioned, throne- like leather chair frowning. "You see when we was little niggas, a bitch like that would've never been hired to report the news." The middle aged man turned his coal black eyes away from the large, flat screen television to a man a few years his senior. A small smoking table sat between them.

"True that. Ted Koppel never made jokes or gave his opinion on what he was reporting," Precious Pete agreed.

He was commonly referred to as "The Gentleman" because of his articulate nature and disdain for profanity. A well-preserved black man with a slicked back coif of frosty hair, Precious Pete was well-dressed in unseasonable but fashionable grey tweed, loafers, gold cuff links, a white shirt, and red tie.

"This is the third one of my guys to be gunned down, and in broad daylight no less. It's highly disappointing," Pete grumbled. "Ross was an important asset of mine. Who would pull off something like this?"

"Well you know what they say. Drugs kill," Black Pop's purple-black skin shined beneath the ceiling lights as he spoke. Precious Pete frowned and began vigorously tapping his foot.

"In case I need to remind you Black. Drugs are our profession. Your job is simple…maintain a peaceful equilibrium between my New York and Chicago assets. Make sure they don't kill each other and that all deliveries are made on time." Precious Pete, cautiously upset with Black Pop's dismissive attitude.

9

"See, I disagree with that statement man." A broad smile spread across Black Pops face. "Your business is drugs. Mine is killing. I left that drug shit alone in the late 80s. I was destroying too many lives - families you see?"

"And now?" Precious Pete inquired sarcastically. "Are you saying you're not destroying lives now? The only reason I'm sitting here today is to have you hunt down whoever is killing my point men. That is what you do…right?"

"True, true." Black Pops' smile remained, though there was something foreboding in his eyes that rubbed Precious Pete the wrong way. "I kill for a living or rather I have others kill for me. But…we only kill niggas who choose to live this hustle lifestyle. Drugs on the other hand - drugs don't give a fuck who it takes down. Dealing that 'New Crop' shit, I can't say I'm mad your niggas are dropping like flies. I try to tell these niggas it ain't the 80's no more. They need to keep that shit off the streets and out of the community."

"A benevolent killer? You never cease to amaze me Black," there was a nervous edge to Precious Pete's voice. His eyes began to dart around the room as though searching for a hidden assailant.

"You know how I feel about that drug shit Double P," Black Pops declared sourly. "I do what I do because it provides an essential service to the streets - cleaning up the trash. I ain't about peddling self-destruction no more. What you do over in Chi Town ain't got nothin' to do with me here up north. I withhold judgment and you know it DP. But when it comes to NYC, my slice of the city, then we have a major problem. And lately. That problem has been getting out-of-hand.

"Well, I say there's money to be made up north, but I won't argue with your naiveté," Precious Pete acknowledged with light scorn. Ignoring the insult, Black Pops flashed a knowing grin at the dapper elder. Just then, in a rush, the homeless man entered the cedar wood paneled room, behind him, a plump, older, dark-skinned woman cursed loudly.

"Nobody told yo ass to kill that muthafucking baby!" She yelled. "He was a baby nigga! A baby! And it's all ova the news!"

Mig

"Yo, that lil nigga took aim at me! I didn't have a choice," the homeless man retorted as he loosened the crumpled plastic hood and bandana to reveal a bright-skinned, boyishly, handsome man with dead copper eyes. A spray of brown freckles fell across the narrow bridge of his nose as well as a dusting on his cheeks. His jaw was square and masculine; his hairline shaped to precision, short cropped and nappy red.

Precious Pete's grip tightened on his cigar as he turned around. Knowingly, Black Pops continued to grin.

"You mean to tell me that was your work?" Precious Pete asked. He nervously pointed at the television screen.

"Yes," Black Pops confirmed. Next, he introduced the two men, "Red, Pete. Pete, Red."

"So this was a Killa Cartel hit?" Precious Pete's cigar trembled in his thin, elegant fingers as he turned to face Black Pops.

"Looks like it was," Black Pops clapped, smiling. "I think you know what that means."

"Black!" Precious Pete shrieked as he shakily rose to his feet. "What...what are you doing?" he asked with trembling voice.

12

Unmoved, Black Pops reiterated, "I don't like 'New Crop'. It makes crack look like children's Tylenol. I told you that five years ago when you and Mayor James started shipping that shit up north."

"Mayor James!" The words seemed to catch in Precious Pete's throat. He quickly looked from the handsome bright-skinned youth then back to Black Pops.

"Me and the mayor go way back," said Black Pops, "but I only recently found out he and you were in business together. It's a shame too. He's corrupt as shit, but that's my nigga and I still need him in his position. I don't have any further use for you though. I know you're pissed off because you're about to die but rest assured you won't be alone for long. Your boys will be joining you soon. I understand you brought them with you - apparently for backup."

"You mutha..." Precious Pete didn't have a chance to finish the slur before Red pulled out his Walther PPK, and planted a slug right between "The Gentleman's" eyes.

"Precious Pete! Oh lawd have mercy! Red baby, what you done did!?" The plump woman jumped back and screamed as Pete's body hit the floor.

13

She cried and grabbed at Red but he shook her off, t hen broke down laughing, displaying a row of pearly, manicured teeth. Black Pops joined him in laughter then turned to the wailing woman.

"Calm the fuck down Suga Momma," he ordered, still laughing. "Now that this nigga and Big Ross is outta the way, I can take over the northeast distribution of New Crop and get it off my muthafucking streets. Shit, ain't that what you wanted after what happened to Bobbi J?" Black Pop's look of mirth switched to one of genuine affection. "Them niggas took yo only seed away from you. You should be singing a hymn of joy this nigga is laying here with a hole in his head." He faced Red; "Go clean yourself up boy. You smell like a muthafucking sewer."

Red smiled and left the room, but not before giving Suga Momma a mocking kiss on the cheek to which he received a sharp slap to the back of the head. He chuckled saying, "Love you too big momma," to which he received another whack.

The second he was gone, Suga Momma turned to Black Pops with tears in her eyes. "Now listen hear suga," her voice trembled, as did her plump, pretty face. "That nigga is doing the most. That was some sloppy shit Black. If we ain't careful, he gon' bring the whole muthafucking city down on us."

"Red's alright," Black Pops sniggered as he turned the dead body over with his foot so that Precious Pete's open eyes stared toward the ceiling. "Get Rochelle and them bitches in here to clean this shit up."

"But daddy! That nigga killed a baby," pressed Suga Momma.

"Bitch, didn't I say get this shit cleaned up?"
"I ain't gon' be too many of your muthafucking bitches Black!" Suga Momma snapped then stomped out of the room.

Chapter 2

Red entered the private locker room Black Pops held for him on reserve, shedding the fermenting rags he himself had smeared with garbage and piss in preparation for killing his mark; he really got into his work. At twenty-three, he was dedicated to the only job he had held since he had been on his own at the age of eleven - a killer. He was good at it, sometimes even enjoyed it.

He cracked his neck from side-to-side then stretched his arms high above his head while inhaling deeply. His muscles were sore. The remainder of Big Ross's guards had chased him throughout Central Park, forcing him to exert a wealth of energy. Currently, the news was reporting the four bodies found. They had yet to discover the nine others strewn throughout the park grounds.

"Hey Red," came a voice sweet as raw honey. A girl, Hershey's special dark, five nine, with a thick and curvy athletic frame stole into the locker room, and leaned against the door.

She wore a strapless, blue Pringle of Scotland stretch mini with matching blue suede stilettos, batting her dark mascara, cat-like eyes at him while she licked her glossed lips.

"Yo! You ain't supposed to be in here Tanasha," said Red looking her up and down. Tanasha Black was a pretty girl - not a beauty in the classic sense. Yet, like many a celebrity, hair and makeup worked wonders. She twirled a strand of her shoulder-length, honey blond weave with a finger while eying the impressive length dangling between his legs.

"I know nigga, why you acting like a bitch though!?" She said and pulled the second-skin blue dress over her head to reveal thick titties and thighs that were lightly oiled and glowing under the florescent lighting. "You ain't supposed to be fucking me either," she continued. "But you about to." She tossed the dress aside, dropped to her knees, took Red's girth into her coco soft hands, and gave it a gentle lick.

"If Pops knew you was in here," Red said, his dick getting hard despite his guise of apprehension. He and Tanasha had played this game for years now.

She repeatedly deep throated him while rubbing the hood of her clit with her middle finger. She pulled off, slapping herself in the face with him fully erect, and laughed.

"It ain't like he can do shit nigga, even if he did know, which he probably does. What! You scared of the nigga?" Red pulled her to her feet and pushed her back up against the door, pressing his chiseled chest against her buoyant D cups.

"Yo, chill with that," he said sticking his tongue into her mouth. He dipped his body low, lining himself up with her, then stood, sliding his dick between her wet pussy lips. She moaned.

"You always on some plotting shit yo," he breathed into her ear as he thrust upwards and deeper into her.

"Can't hate a bitch for being ambitious," Tanasha exhaled then inhaled. She had been fucking Red since they were twelve and thirteen. It still kinda hurt like it was her first time. "Black ain't never been no daddy to me. Plus he killed my momma; I can give a fuck what he think." She lifted her leg, prompting him to hold it in the air and fuck her in that position.

"You don't know that for sure," cautioned Red.

"My Aunt Delores wouldn't have lied to me Red. Once I get absolute proof, I'm settin’ shit off! She knew yo daddy too. She say she know some shit that'll make you wanna put a cap in his ass quick! Now turn me around!" She commanded while lowering her leg. Wet with her juices, Red pulled his near eleven inches out of her, and roughly turned her around, her fat ass cheeks pressed hard against him. He dipped, then re-entered her, pumping harder from behind.

"I'm telling you son. Me and you would make a bangin’ ass team," said Tanasha, her breasts pressed hard against the door. "I mean what the fuck he got us doing anyway? Taking out ballers so he can take over their operations just to shut them down! It's bullshit baby. We should be taking over they shit for ourselves! What the fuck I care about a muthafucka gettin' high?"

"I like what Pops is about," Red responded. "Killing criminals is a good thing. Distributing New Crop - not so much."

"Nigga, there’s mad money to be made. Even Chandler thinks so,"

Tanasha responded through several deep breaths. Red had quickened the pace; he was really pounding her now.

"What the fuck Chandler know about the trap game? I could ask you the same shit ma!"

"He's head of security! A position you should have accepted; and he ain't a dumb nigga. He knows what's up. Once all these niggas are dead, new ones will pop up in their place and start making that dough. Why shouldn't we control them? Listen Red, I'ma need you on my side when shit go down."

"I told you to chill with that shit Tanasha. You trynna get me killed? Ain't it enough that we together?" He rested his chin on her shoulder; they were both sweating. "Ain't it enough I give you this good dick?"

"Me and how many other bitches Red? Don't try to play like you love a bitch," she pouted. Red squeezed both her ass cheeks and began grinding deep inside her.

"Don't be that way T, you know this dick is yours and yours only," he lied sweetly. Tanasha knew he wasn't telling the truth. Even so, as far as she knew, and as complicated as their clandestine affair/relationship was, she was the only one who had his heart.

She would bleed a bitch slow before she let him go. "Do you really mean that Red?" She purred.

"No doubt ma...within reason," he corrected himself. Tanasha laughed. "One of these days you gon' have to give into me Red. You gonna have to give me what I want."

"And what's that ma?"

"Killa Cartel."

Chapter 3

Black Pops sat comfortably watching television in a barely furnished suite of Times Square's W hotel. At six foot five, he was a stick of a man. Purple black skin, with a crown of immaculate jet black waves; he had the face of a handsome jackal and the instincts of a beast of prey. His Killa Cartel was the stuff of urban legend in New York City. Niggas were known to disappear and never be heard from again if the price was right and he willed it so. He, himself remained a shadowy figure in NYC's underground crime world. Instead of hustling the streets like he did in his youth, he preferred to strengthen his ties with those in the upper echelon of society - friends in high places. The most important being the only other person in the room with him, the city's Republican Mayor, Randolph James.

Dirty Red: A Killa's Love Story

"Under Mayor Randolph James's stewardship, New York City has experienced a rise in crime and drug related violence not seen since the height of the crack epidemic," roared a pigmy-sized woman from the television screen. She stood before a lectern on the steps of Manhattan's City Hall.
Her lilac pants suit, short black hair, and mini double chin, all fluttered in the early evening wind as she slammed down a clinched fist.

"We as New Yorkers cannot! Will not! Go back to a time where our murder rate rivaled that of Chicago's," she continued. "I challenge Mayor James to bring young Tamar Mitgowen's murderer to justice.
I challenge Mayor James to rid our streets of the New Crop, a heinous concoction of heroin, crack cocaine, salvia, ketamine, and God knows what else! It's addicting the city's minority youth at alarming rates, and tearing families apart!" She paused to catch her breath. Her Asiatic/Hispanic features softened from its fiery grimace; she suddenly became calm and motherly. "I can promise you as Mayor of New York City, I will not rest until senseless murders like this are a thing of the past.

23

I can't rest now! And you as citizens shouldn't either."
She bowed her head as a single tear slid down her
powdered cheek.

"Damn that bitch good ain't she?" Black Pops
declared as he excitedly clapped his hands. There was
light applause as Luca De Ha Miller waved from the 56
inch flat screen that hung from the wall like an animated
family portrait. "Now I see why she won the Democratic
primary last week to challenge yo ass. What you gon'
do?" He asked with a teasing grin. Mayor Randolph
James grimaced as he nervously paced the hotel room.
He turned to face Black Pops, trying his best to look in
control.

"Just whose fucking side are you on?" He
snapped. Hollow cheeked with a narrow crag for a nose
and piercing blue eyes, the well-dressed Caucasian man
nervously ran his hand through his slick of silver fox hair
and gritted his teeth. "Luca De Ha Miller isn't the
problem," he said. "The problem is you motherfuckers
starting fires all over the city that I have to put out!"

"What muthafucking fire did I start nigga?" Smiled Black Pops.

"Are you going to tell me you didn't have anything to do with this?" Mayor James pointed at Tamar Mitgowen's image on the screen as though it were a credible accusing witness. "You don't think I know how much it benefits you now that Big Ross and Precious Pete are out of the picture?"

"You know I stopped fucking with that drug game a long time ago Randy. That's your department. So don't blame me because some muthafucka fucking with your bottom line," said Black Pops.

"I don't need this shit!" The Mayor retorted. "Especially one day before my annual art gala! I look like a fucking idiot! You're supposed to be my ear to the streets and warn me beforehand about shit like this!"

Black Pops shrugged. "Nigga, you got enough ears on the muthafucking streets slanging that nasty shit for you! How do I know you didn't order the hits? With both them niggas dead, you control all the New Crop in the state!"

"I'm just the middle man and you know it!"
Cursed the Mayor.

"Shiiiit, maybe I'm next on your list? It would
look real good for your tough on crime re-election
campaign," Black Pops absently gnawed the butt of his
cigar while watching the screen as the Democratic
candidate for Mayor shook hands with a group of
supporters.

"That's absolutely ridiculous Dessard," Mayor
James protested. "You and I go back way too far."

Dessard Lucas was Black Pops' government
label, and yes, he and Mayor James went back decades.
They formed a brotherhood of sorts while serving in the
2nd Ranger Battalion of the U.S. Army's RD Force,
during Reagan's 1983 Invasion of Grenada. When they
returned to civilian life, they both pursued local politics
in their respective NYC districts.

James, a conservative, well connected, and
well…white, excelled and won several seats on his way
to becoming Mayor.

Dessard Lucas didn't fare as well. Notwithstanding his impressive military record, he was a mediocre politician with very little support from his district. Hence, he became a well-versed street hustler who kept his foot in the door of the city's political establishment by doing the dirty work for James and other power players.

"This will blow over," offered Black Pops. "Having those niggas off the street will benefit us both in the long run." He was enjoying watching the Mayor squirm.

"Read the fucking tea leaves Dessard! This shit ain't blowing over no time soon! And this Miller bitch is gonna make this fucking gangster's dead kid the center of her election platform! No, this isn't going away! It's just beginning! I have 13 dead bodies waiting for me. I need something! I need something big and you're gonna help me!"

"How?" Asked Black Pops with skepticism.

"I want the nigga who did this! You hear! I want him and I know you know where to get him. Give him up to me and I can make it a life-changing event for you Dessard."

"Since when do I work for you Randy? You the muthafucking public servant. Nigga, you work for me," barked Black Pops indignantly.

"If I were the one who caught him," Mayor James continued hungrily, "They'll come out to Gracie Mansion and celebrate me like they did when Obama caught Bin Laden. Otherwise, this could sink my candidacy. If that happens, things would soon become very inconvenient for both of us."

"Why not just take out the little Mexican bitch?" Asked Black Pops.

"What!? For one, she's from goddamned Puerto Rico. And two, it's that type of thinking that has us standing here in the first place!" Yelled Mayor James.

"I don't give a fuck if the bitch is Fort Apache the Bronx, American Indian. If you ain't re-elected, I'm out of a lot of cover and a lot of money!" Yelled Black Pops.

"Then give me the muthafucka who did this," Mayor James requested, taking a seat across from Black Pops. "I can get you on the City Council," he added.

"Something small in the beginning with room for growth. Be smart Dessard and think about it...the path to legitimacy you always wanted. Just turn over the shooter. I'll handle the rest."

"And what? You expect him not to talk," Black Pops cursed inwardly knowing he had just confirmed Mayor James' accusations and quickly tried to recover. "That is if I can dig up some information on the streets," he hastily added.

"My people will cut his tongue out. Make it look like retaliation from Ross's family," explained Mayor James. He stood then walked toward the exit leaving Black Pops with a, "Get it done! Both our asses are on the line because of this mess!"

Black Pops smiled, turning his attention back to the television screen.

Mig

Chapter 4

Red slowly opened his eyes and yawned. He felt
safe and at peace. It was always that way when she was
around. He glanced down at the dark-haired girl, who
was lightly snoring, sprawled across his chest and buried
his nose deep in her wavy tresses. She smelled like fresh
cucumber, lavender, and lime, a smell he had grown to
love just as much as he did her.

"Aleide," he whispered and smiled. She stirred
just a bit, the warm touch of her skin against his caused
him to stir down below. Aleide yawned softly then
sighed.

"Good morning," she cooed looking up into his
dark eyes with her own hazel green jewels. Red leaned
forward and kissed her.

"Morning baby. You sleep well?" He asked as he
stroked her fragrant hair. Aleide smiled warmly.

"Wonderfully," she answered and then yelled,
"Jamarcus! Why didn't you wake me?" She sat up
quickly and delivered a soft punch to his chest.

"I'm going to be late for work," she smiled, skipping from the ivory and teak king sized bed, over to the large bedroom's adjoining bathroom.

Red smiled, watching her nude, lithe body disappear behind the bathroom's heavy oak door. He met Aleide two years ago, purely accidental if not by fate, which Red chose to believe was the latter. He had just finished a job, escaping via a downtown six train. His thoughts were consumed with the murder he had just committed when he noticed her sitting across from him.

She was a petite, disarmingly pretty little thing. Her shining chestnut hair fell just past her shoulders and framed her soft chin, heart shaped lips, pert nose, and full cheeks. Large, doe-shaped eyes lay sheltered beneath a rush of black lashes that curled upward like a dancing flame. Her lean arms were pale against her navy t-shirt. However, the size of her silver dollar nipples was unmistakable beneath the dark fabric. Her form-fitting jeans were chalky grey and accentuated the curve of her slender legs.

Red smiled, or almost smiled, it was more of a friendly scowl. The girl appeared to acknowledge the gesture with a polite averting of the eyes down to her lap.

After a few seconds, she looked back up. Red was still scowling.

"What are you looking at?" He asked, feigning annoyance.

"Excuse me, are you talking to me?" The girl inquired, perplexed.

"Of course! Who else would I be talking to," he said.

"Well, I wasn't looking at you," she responded. "In fact, I think you were looking at me."

"So what if I was. Yo I'm...," He fell silent for a moment and then, "I'm Red. And you are?"

Smiling coyly, the girl shook her head. "I'm sure your mother didn't name you Red," but was uncertain as to why she had made the announcement. Although she thought he had a nice smile, he definitely wasn't her type. Much too rugged she reflected.

Regardless of his seemingly permanent scowl, Red smiled. He was undeniably handsome, knew it, and didn't mind correcting his frown to throw on the charm for the ladies.

"Jamarcus; my mom's named me Jamarcus." Red looked at her expectantly. The girl looked back down at her hands and remained silent as though she was done with the budding conversation.

"I don't mean to come on strong or come off rude," he continued, "but I don't usually talk to girls on the train. Actually, I don't really talk to anybody much."

It was true. Red was a loner by occupational design and had rarely met women spontaneously. What with his sister, Tammy running the Northern Tip brothel and working for Black Pops, women had been more or less provided for him since he was twelve or thirteen. Then there was the ever watchful eye of Tanasha, his only girlfriend, if you could call her that. She ensured he never got attached to any of the said provided women. In essence, Red was used to fucking and leaving.

"Aleide," offered the girl with the cautious look of jumping off a cliff with a bungee cord tied around her ankle. "My name is Aleide," she repeated with a shy smile.

"A lady," Red repeated, turning the name over in his head several times. After a silent moment he smiled, "It's pretty, A lady," he said. "What kinda name is that?"

33

"It's Portuguese. My family is from Brazil."

"Aww shit, I thought you was Puerto Rican or something," he laughed.

"You're very charming," she frowned, seemingly turned off. Red waited for her to follow up but she didn't.

The two rode in silence for several seconds before he spoke again.

"So can I take you out some time?" He asked.

"I don't go out with thugs," Aleide rolled her eyes.

"I ain't a thug. What about me is thug?" Asked Red. By now, he was patting down his gear, which consisted of a fitted, black v-neck cashmere, grey slacks, and black loafers. He looked like he worked in Banana Republic, or somewhere more high-end. Aleide brought a clear polished, finely manicured finger up to her eyes.

"It's all in the eyes papi. I have five brothers, and no matter how nice they clean up, they all have eyes like you," she said. Red detected a trace of bitterness in her voice that made him wonder what pain she had experienced. Made him a ant to protect her.

Smiling, he suddenly got up, crossed over, and took the seat beside her.

"I mean I gets busy if I need to," he spoke quietly. "But I'ma good dude ma and trust me, none of yo brothers are like me he countered."

"I don't like it when boys call me ma," Aleide informed him, casting a net.

"Well luckily I'ma man and I won't ever call you ma again beautiful. I just want to spend some time with you, get to know you. This may be a once in a lifetime chance for both of us," he whispered in her ear.

"Once in a lifetime chance for what?" Aleide managed to say. Her flushed cheeks betrayed her arousal from his warm breath on her ear. Red smiled, noting her hardening nipples.

"Let's find out," he said. Aleide didn't answer right away. When she spoke next, it was only to tell him her train stop was approaching. They remained silent for the remainder of their short time together.

She stood, walked to the door at the 14th Street Union Square stop, and waited for it to open. Without looking back, she called out her phone number. Red immediately fumbled for his phone, eagerly tapping the digits into the keypad.

Mig

"Now you gon' have every nigga on the train calling you," he teased as the doors closed. Aleide laughed, embarrassed as he waved goodbye to her blurring image.

"Can you put on some coffee?" Red's thoughts were wrestled back to the present as Aleide's voice floated in from beneath a running shower in the bathroom.

"A'ight!" He made his way down a dim corridor of polished cedar into a small, pre-war designed kitchen.

The morning headlines were dominated by the death of Big Ross and his son, Tamar, along with eleven henchmen found spread out over Central Park, all with single gunshots to the dome. Groggy eyed, Red settled down at a small table with a copy of the daily news. "ENOUGH!" Was written in large, bold font across the front page in bright red ink. A picture of young Tamar Mitgowen was layered beneath it. Red tossed the paper aside; it landed on the floor, displaying a two-page spread with an aerial photo of the park. Small red x's marked the various locations where the thirteen bodies were discovered.

"Why didn't you wake me up?" Aleide entered the kitchen wearing one of Red's oversized t-shirts, her wet hair wrapped in a damp towel.

"I like watching you sleep. You still have about ten minutes before you have to bounce," Red motioned for her to take the seat across from him. For him, she was his little oasis of peace and normalcy.

"Here you go. Just like you like it," he slid a steaming mug of coffee across the table. Aleide smiled but it quickly became a grimace as her eyes fell on the discarded newspaper on the floor.

"My God! Thirteen dead!" She shouted. "How could someone kill a baby in cold blood like that? I don't care what kind of criminal the father was. I hope they catch the son of a bitch and hang him!"

Red sipped his coffee as she picked up the paper and glanced over the aerial photo. He harbored a guilty sense of pride regarding his work, but realized their relationship would be over if she knew he was the perpetrator. As far as Aleide knew, Red worked accounting at a small tech startup business that was in the midst of experiencing serious growth. In her mind, he was one of the good guys, a hood success story.

One day he would leave it all behind; take her away somewhere far from New York City, and start a family. At least that's what she told herself. Had she been aware of his actual occupation, she would have realized individuals in that trade rarely made it to retirement.

Red's thoughts were interrupted by his phone vibrating loudly against the tiled countertop. He excused himself and picked up the call only to hear Black Pops voice crackling into his ears.

"I need you at the Outhouse downtown," he said. "Yesterday's theatrics in the park was sloppy as shit, but got shit popping as planned."

"Sounds good!" Red replied then walked out of the kitchen leaving Aleide alone to read.

"There are a couple of loose ends with Pete's peoples I need you to handle," said Black Pops. "He came into town yesterday with his sons and a small army. I'ma have to put you and Heiress to work."

"You know I work better alone Pops," Red reminded him somewhat sourly.

Dirty Red: A Killa's Love Story

"Heiress's wet game is as sick as yours," said Black Pops. Red remained silent. Heiress was another one of Black Pops' wet men, second only to Red in number of kills. The two enjoyed a friendly competition with a lot of sexual tension in between.
Black Pops continued, "I need you to get on down to the Outhouse. Chandler will be there to brief both of you."

"Why the Outhouse?" Red asked warily.

"Muthafucka would you prefer an email?" Black Pops cursed.

"My bad Pops. I guess I'm a little on edge with all the publicity and shit."

"That's what happens when you put a hole in a toddler's head?" He snapped.

"I wish it hadn't gone down like that," Red sighed.

"It was sloppy Red, Black Pops said fuming. You know better than that!" "But it is what it is. Take the train down to the Outhouse. It'll be quicker than driving."

"On my way," Red grumbled, uneasy with being told how to navigate his city.

Mig

In truth, he would have taken the subway as opposed to drive anyway, feeling somewhat uneasy about the amount of media attention his last job was receiving. Though they would be hard-pressed to link him to the crime, he didn't want to risk any traffic stops by the police. Now fully dressed, Aleide entered the living room. "Baby, I'm outta here." Kissing him on the cheek, she inquired "is everything alright?"

"Yeah, just some bullshit at work I have to deal with," he told her as he placed his hands on her waist and pulled her into him.

"You know I love you, right?" He said. Aleide stood on her toes and threw her arms around his neck. For a moment, the two became lost in one another's eyes.

"I love you too Jamarcus; don't ever doubt it" she said, then softly kissed him goodbye.

Chapter 5

Red showered and quickly dressed. Leaving his Riverside Drive apartment, he walked several blocks over to Broadway where he took the number 2 train downtown. He easily found a seat as the train was less crowded than he expected. Right away, he noticed several people reading both the Post and Daily News. Young Tamar Mitgowen's first grade school photo was splashed across both covers.

A gnawing feeling of guilt crept through him, *It was either him or me,* he told himself. Nevertheless, the feeling remained.

The Outhouse was Killa Cartel's base of operations. It was located in a block of abandoned warehouses in Manhattan's Lower East Side. Black Pops had acquired the space years ago when he was still running drugs and used it as a distribution point. Currently, what he distributed was death to drug runners and the like.

"It's about time you got here." Chandler Saint jean stepped aside as Red entered the mahogany boardroom.

A 12 foot long onyx stone table separated the narrow space down the middle and was surrounded by comfortable Aeron leather desk chairs. The corporate-like appearance was a far cry from the dilapidated warehouse he had entered.

Red sucked his teeth as Black Pops' head of security eyed him down. At 6 foot 3 inches and a solid 230 pounds, Chandler wasn't a handsome man, but not unattractive either. He looked somewhat like Terry Crews and Terrence Howard mixed in a Petri dish and set out to bake in the sun. Additionally, he was stylish, wearing a charcoal Givenchy suit with a statement red tie, and black Gucci slides on his feet. His opulent, Cartier gold encrusted diamond earrings reflected prisms of color on the wall when caught by the light.

"Looks like I'm the first one here," Red stated while taking a seat near the head of the table.

"The rest of the click will be here in a minute," Chandler responded. His short, black waves were sculpted to perfection but marred by a white piece of lint which caused Red to smile.

He always noticed things like that, tiny details that pulled back the curtain on the pretense of being untouchable. "Where's Pops?" Red asked.

"He's on his way," Chandler said. Up to this point, he had yet to take a seat.

"The old man sounded pissed off with me," Red offered. Chandler rolled his eyes and laughed.

"When is that nigga never pissed off about something. You're good though. You just have a lot of cleanup work ahead of you today."

"He said Precious Pete's kid has an army of niggas here. If Pops is mad about me bodying all those niggas yesterday..."

"We didn't know Pete showed up with so much backup," Chandler interrupted.

"Why not? Isn't it your job to know shit like that," Red queried. Chandler simply sighed.

"There's a lot of shit that's been going down behind the scenes that you aren't privy to Red."

"You still didn't answer my question," griped Red. Before he could get another word out, Black Pops entered the room with Tanasha behind him.

"Don't give my nigga none of yo shit Red," said Black Pops. A cigar hung from his mouth like an ornament left on the lawn well past the holiday season. "You the muthafucka that got the whole city up in arms over killing that boy."

"I didn't plan on killing a kid," spat Red. "The nigga was about to..."

"You ain't gotta explain that shit Red. Daddy know what's up," Tanasha spoke up on his behalf. Chandler gave her a cool look, cleared his throat then announced, "The shit still don't look good on paper. But it was a necessary evil. I'm sure Red is filled with remorse."

Red didn't like the sarcastic tone in Chandler's voice and made a mental note to check him on it later.

The sound of high heels clicking across the floor alerted everyone to the arrival of Heiress. Heiress King was a self-proclaimed "Bad Bitch." Standing five foot nine, she was built thick, but lean in all the right places. She offset her milk chocolate skin and model looks with a boy cut platinum bob - worn long in the front it covered one eye like couture pirate wear.

Wrapped in a black, second skin cat suit, tan Uggs, and a flowing camel overcoat, she paused..."What the fuck all y'all niggas staring at?" She asked as all eyes were on her.

"Maybe it's because you look like yo ass about to go to a goddamn photo shoot instead of settin' shit off," laughed Chandler. Heiress rolled her eyes with a smile.

"You know I gots to look good my nigga." She walked pass him, nodded to Tanasha then stopped in front of Red.

"That was some fucked up shit you pulled yesterday Red," she scolded.

In a teasing manner, Red stated "Fall back ma, don't be mad 'cause I'm stacking up numbers and you ain't."

"Yeah nigga, my numbers would be as high as yours if I was taking out little kids," Heiress bit back while delivering a soft tap to the side of his head.

"Ok, ok," interrupted Black Pops, "Enough of the bullshit. We got some serious business to discuss instead of y'all muthafuckas comparing dick sizes."

"I win in that department," quipped Red, laughing. Tanasha nodded in agreement and shot her father a nasty look.

"Listen! We got a problem," admonished Black Pops.

"More specifically, retaliation for yesterday's melee in Central Park," Chandler stated while eyeing Red.

"Has Killa Cartel been mentioned?" Heiress asked. "I wouldn't imagine so as our reputation excludes such sloppiness." She seated herself next to Red with a playful sneer.

"As a matter of fact, our name has come up," Chandler continued. "Fortunately, Black Pops commands a certain amount of respect on the streets so no one has dared bring it to his doorstep. Our priorities are to take out niggas talking, as well as anyone from either Ross's or Pete's camp who figure they're owed revenge.

Tanasha asked, "Why was Ross under such heavy guard? I mean, since when did that nigga start rolling deep like that?"

"I was wondering the same thing," Heiress added.

"Whatever his reasons for increased security, you should have just capped his ass and bounced!" Black Pops said while pointing an accusing finger at Red. "But naw! Yo ass wanna play cowboys and muthafucking Indians. Now we got Pete's boys, Pretty Piper, and Fine Felix up here ready to link up with Lil Reggie and the rest of Big Ross's people."

"Well that's why we're here," Red said, now outwardly pissed. "So what we gotta do to fix it?"

"You know what you have to do!" Black Pops countered. "Take those niggas out!"

"Pete's body is at Sam's Mortuary. I have word both Piper and Felix are on their way to pick it up. I want you two," he pointed to Red and Heiress, "To ambush 'em and take 'em out. Chandler and Tanasha will handle Lil Reggie and his momma. I want clean kills. None of that cowboy shit from yesterday."

Tanasha asked, "And then what? We take these niggas out? Take over their operations and shut the shit down? I don't get it. For one, there's money to be made and killing these niggas is not gon' keep New Crop out the city. So we might as well control it. Killa Cartel should come out of the shadows..."

"Shut the fuck up Tanasha!" Black Pops interrupted. "I had yo ass trained to kill not advise me on what the fuck I'm about."

"You think these niggas gon' just let it rest? Some new niggas will move right on in, then what? We gon' run up on them in the dark too?"

"Listen here Tanasha," cautioned Black Pops.

"What the fuck you gon' do? Spank me?" Tanasha challenged.
Black Pops rested his face in his hands moaning. "Chandler, can you escort Judas here outta the muthafucking room!" Chandler stood on command and walked over to Tanasha.

"What, you kicking me out the meeting?" She looked at her father with shock but he kept his face buried in his palms, ignoring her. "Daddy! Da...oh no you didn't."

"Please Ms. Black," Chandler said cordially. Tanasha quickly stood, brushed him aside, and made her way to the door. She turned back with fire in her eyes, stating, "I bet you this Robin Hood shit blow right up in your face! Then come see me!"

She stormed through the door with Chandler close on her heels. Once in the privacy of the outside corridor, he grabbed Tanasha by her arm then pushed her against the wall.

"What the fuck was that shit back there?" He asked. "That was way off what we been talking about baby. Don't fuck up our plans on some emotional shit."

"Nigga please! What moves are you making? All you do is talk about shit! But I don't see you doing shit. I didn't see you standing up and saying you agree with me!"

Chandler pressed her against the wall then pressed his lips to hers.

She responded, slipping her tongue into his mouth. They kissed for several seconds before Chandler pulled away, breathing hard. "Because it would be like treason in his eyes," he informed her. "I think he's doing all this wanna clean up the streets shit because he never made it in politics. He thinks he's healing the streets by killing assassins. What he doesn't recognize is we're hired by those same killers to execute murderers they don't like. He's no better than the scum he wants us to take out."

"At least we know it!" Tanasha, happy to have someone in her corner.

"Just like you said, we might as well rule it," Chandler agreed. He took out a red iPhone C then handed it to her. "I'm building with niggas in distribution on both ends. I've been prepping them for us baby. You just gotta stick to the plan and work on Red. We need him ready by tonight. This oughta give him the push we need."

Taking the phone, Tanasha looked it over. She asked, "What's on it?"

After Chandler keyed in the phone's code, the home screen displayed. With a few swipes of the finger, a video began playing. Tanasha's eyes got big like she was watching a resurrection.

"That, along with what I told you about his pops, should put him in the right mindset," Chandler smiled.

"Yo! How did you get this shit?" She asked excited.

"I have my ways baby girl. Just make sure he sees it."

"No doubt, but hey, see if you can get me put back on our assignment," she said.

"After your performance, not a chance. You may have genuinely gained his mistrust in there. It's best you chill - lay low."

"Ok baby. I'm sorry, you know how I get sometimes." Tanasha kissed his lips softly.

"It's cool, just chill. Let me get back in there before he starts asking questions," Chandler advised while backing away.

"You do that," said Tanasha, smiling, "because I'm sho' the fuck gon' do me," she mumbled under her breath then removed her phone to place a call.

Chapter 6

Red and Heiress made their way back uptown to Sam's Mortuary in Heiress's platinum and chrome fitted 2015 Escalade, a ride far too flashy for Red's taste. A few years older than Red, the two went back almost as far as he and Tanasha. Upon their first meeting, they struck an immediate love/hate camaraderie. Unlike Tanasha, who had the world handed to her on a silver platter, Red and Heiress shared the same pain of losing their parents to crime and crack as well as a connection most others in Killa Cartel couldn't touch.

Heiress parked the immaculate ride two blocks from their target, they quickly made their way on foot, and snuck in through a back window after reaching the mortuary. They could hear arguing as they slowly approached the front of the business. In order to listen to the voices, Heiress halted her advancement, then raised her hand, signaling for Red to do the same. There was a squabble going on indeed between the owner of the mortuary and someone they made out to be Pretty Piper, who was Precious Pete's eldest.

"I told you we got shit handled old man. You'll be paid handsomely for your service," Piper said in a nasally, snide tone of voice.

"I don't care about the money Mr. Pretty. I don't like all these men walking around here with weapons. Y'all look like you ready to start a war up in here. I'm sorry, but you have to take the body and leave now. Please sir," the mortuary owner's voice broke.

"We'll leave as soon as the niggas who did this to my daddy show up. Don't worry, I got word they're on their way as we speak."

Red looked across to Heiress mouthing the words, "What the fuck?" She shook her head indicating her surprise as well.

"I don't want any killing going on here Mr. Pretty. This is a simple place of business."

"Can you shut this shook nigga up please," another man entered the front parlor. "Them niggas oughta be here any minute. I got Terence and his crew in the cut covering the entrance, Macky and Jamal are checking the back."

53

Mig

Heiress winked at Red and began creeping forward. Even in their current circumstances, Red smiled. Heiress was one fine broad who knew how to handle a gat like no one else he had ever met, and was always ready to throw down. He followed her lead as she crept up to the side opening arch of the parlor. Before he could get into proper position, she rolled into the parlor like a ball of yarn, simultaneously letting off multiple shots. Pretty Piper, the mortuary proprietor, and Red determined the other man was Fine Felix due to his strong resemblance to Precious Pete, all scrambled.

Felix ran, flung himself through the nearest window, crash landing outside. Instantaneously, he was on his feet, his gat pointed through the broken glass, and releasing rounds of ammunition. For several seconds, the air was alive with the sound of gunfire. Red and Heiress had already backed out of the parlor and were in the midst of taking on several men who were entering the backdoor.

Fine Felix was joined in the front of the mortuary by seven of his men. He had them flank him from both sides as he hurriedly made his way back around to the front entrance. Kicking in the door, he came through blasting.

After the smoke cleared, he was greeted with the sight of the bullet ridden bodies of his younger brother and the proprietor sprawled on the floor in a sea of blood.

"Not so pretty anymore, huh!" Red called out as he rushed Felix, taking him to the ground. Fine Felix's men didn't have the opportunity to assist him because Heiress was close to the floor, letting lead fly, catching niggas in ankles, calves, and shins. Felix who was stronger than Red had anticipated the move, broke free of his grip, delivering Red a stiff blow to his jaw. Red fell back onto the floor, but quickly recovered by sweeping his leg to the side, knocking Felix's feet from beneath him and forcing him to the floor as well.

"We gotta make moves!" Heiress shouted while backing out of the parlor as Fine Felix scrambled back over to the window and desperately lunged outside.

Red sprung to his feet to give chase, but found himself dodging gunfire from two of the surviving men Heiress had downed. However, she was quick to correct her mistake, putting slugs in the back of their heads. Red skipped over the bodies and covered Heiress's back as she charged past dead bodies toward the back exit.

"I hope you counting nigga!" She called back to Red.

"You got a long way to go before you catch up to me shorty," Red laughed. "We can trade numbers when we get out of this bitch alive!" He could hear running feet behind them. Not only were they outnumbered, they were also outgunned. Nevertheless, they had both survived worse ordeals.

"You got smoke?" Heiress called back desperately.

"Yeah one!" Red answered.

"Then use it," she yelled then kicked through the back door shooting first. Red tossed a small gunmetal canister behind him; it automatically exploded into a choking cloud of tear gas.

56

He and Heiress hopped a rusted fence behind the mortuary and ran through a shrub-filled backyard, eventually emerging on the opposite street, which was a tree-lined block of Brownstones and brick apartment co-ops.

"Break left! Red said. Heiress followed close behind as they covered the block, exiting onto Amsterdam Ave.

"Fuck my ride," Heiress exclaimed. "For all we know, that bitch could be rigged too!"

"What?" Red yelled, breathing hard. Within the past twenty-four hours, he had survived a death sprint and had been afforded a second chance at life.

"You heard that nigga!" Heiress continued. "Somebody tipped them off we were coming. Them niggas was armed up deep. We were just lucky we got the drop on them before they did us."

The two of them cleared four blocks in less than ninety seconds. They decided against taking the subway and stuck to the street, blending into the crowd of people.

Red asked, "Who would have set us up and why?" He noticed Heiress's makeup was smeared and her hair frayed.

57

"Who else would pull some shit like this? Maybe all that talk of getting New Crop off the streets is bullshit after all," she grumbled while wrapping her arm around his, and leaning into him like they were an attractive couple out for a stroll. "He filled my head with getting revenge for my momma and daddy with killing these dope boys, but he was taking over they shit the whole time."

"Wait! What the fuck are you talking about?" Red stopped walking, cautiously looked behind him, and then turned to look Heiress directly in the eye that was uncovered by her hair. "You trying to say this was Pops or some shit?"

"Think about it Red," Heiress urged. "Right now he can run the entire east coast crop. Nobody can stop him."

"Yeah, but he shutting that shit down," Red protested. "And you know why!"

"Because of what happened to Cookie, his first wife? How do we know that ain't a bunch of bullshit he made up to manipulate us?

He took us both in when we were kids because our mommas and daddies died behind this drug shit just like Cookie did, but who's to say it's true. This nigga has had us killing for him since we were little!" She argued.

"That's what I'm saying. Yo," Red took her by the arm again and began to move. "We're his best wet men! Plus, he's been like a father to us. Yo, Tanasha been putting shit in your head? You know she's crazy right!?"

"Then why you fucking her?"

"You know about that?" Red sounded surprised.

"Nigga, everybody know, including Pops," Heiress enlightened him.

"So you saying he would roll on us 'cause I'm fucking the daughter that hates him?"

"No. He would roll on us because he wanna take in all that paper," Heiress corrected.

Red stopped walking for a second time. "Naw, it's Tanasha who wants that trap! You saw how she acted this morning," he declared.

"Tanasha is a bad bitch and pussy is her power," Heiress continued. "But she's a dumb bitch too," she said bitterly, "too ambitious for her own good. One thing I do know is she wouldn't snitch on you."

59

"Wait! What are you not telling me yo?"

"We have to call Tanasha first," Heiress replied.

"Why T?" Red asked, not wanting to be caught between a father-daughter battle royale.

"Real talk, she's the last person we need to be calling," hoping Heiress would feel him.

"I know what happened at the Outhouse this morning makes her look shady too, but trust me Red. She's the only person we can call right now.

"Trust will get a nigga killed, ma."

"Or it can keep yo ass alive. Your choice," Heiress declared.

Chapter 7

"Heads up! We got multiple bodies uptown; Captain wants you live." Lae Wein stepped into Detective Lance Brahca's small office and tossed a green, accordion folder on his overcrowded desk. Detective Brahca leaned back in his swivel chair, sighing heavily. He was a weary looking man, in his early forties with a grizzled and grey face that might have passed for handsome if he wasn't worn down by years of intermittent insomnia. He looked the thin Vietnamese woman over with dull eyes.

"Who we talking about this time?" He inquired.

"Peter Rodel, aka Precious Pete. His body turned up in midtown yesterday, single shot to the dome. Apparently, his kid shows up at the 6th Street morgue just after 10 p.m. last night and had his body moved to a spot on 103rd Street. Um…, Sam's Mortuary."

"Who cleared that?" Asked the Detective sitting up at attention.

"No idea but the kid is dead now, along with about seven others, including the mortuary's owner."

61

"You shittin' me, Lae?"

"Massive shoot out. People in the surrounding area are shaken, said it sounded like the Fourth of July out there."

"Any witnesses?" Detective Brahca rose from his seat and began putting on a beige sports jacket.

"That's why the Cap wants us up there," Lae said in response to his question.

"Us? Me - you're staying here."

"Oh come on Lance. You can use me out there. I'm a forensic pathologist!"

"You're a student who one day may become a specialist. As of now, you're my secretary."

"You're a real asshole Lance," she pouted. Detective Brahca took her around the waist, delivering a soft peck on the lips. His crooked pea-sized teeth were coffee and tobacco stained.

"I'm just thinking of your safety Lae," he said in a gruff but soothing voice. With a disappointed sigh, Lae turned away from him.

"Go do what you have to do. I'll be here holding down the fort," she said.

Half an hour later, Detective Brahca was on the gruesome scene. NYPD had the block of 103rd and Amsterdam Ave. closed off from both ends, swarming around the mortuary like worker ants reconstructing their colony after a storm. Standing in the front parlor, Brahca was surrounded by blood, brain matter, and discarded bodies in various death poses. "Who's in charge here?" Holding up his badge for his fellow officers to see.

"That would be me Detective Brahca," said an approaching woman.

Extending her hand, she introduced herself as "Special Agent Lara Spencer." Detective Brahca seemed confused and hesitated several seconds before mirroring the gesture.

"My reputation precedes me," he said looking her over. With skin the hue of silk onyx, she wore a dark suit, tailored to accentuate her healthy curves and expensive heels which caused her to appear to be considerably taller than her five foot six inches.

"You were all over the news last night detective."

Detective Brahca asked, "Do you think there's any connection here with what happened in the park yesterday?"

63

"Not certain. Whoever put a slug in Peter Rodel took time to remove it as well. However, there is a credible connection between him and Ross Mitgowen which leads me to believe that not only are the two connected, but this is just the beginning of something big."

Tanasha pulled up to the corner of 10th Ave. and 86th Street in an all black Tesla Model S bumping Roger and Zapp's "Computer Love." Red frowned, and wondered, *What does she know that Heiress isn't telling me?*

Heiress also looked annoyed as the ride came to a halt before her. Red was quick to open the passenger side door for her to step in. She smiled and batted her lashes, saying, "quite the gentleman," to which he rolled his eyes then jumped into the backseat.

"Uh, why you sitting back there yo?" Tanasha asked.

"Just push the fucking whip and turn that shit down!" Red commanded. Tanasha smacked her lips. "Whateva nigga!" While turning the music volume down, she turned to face Heiress then asked, "So what's good? Why you call me on my burner?"

"We were nearly ambushed at the mortuary," Heiress reported. "Somebody from our side let Pete's boys know we were coming." She stared ahead as she spoke, "I think it was Pops. Red don't believe he would pull some shit like this, but we both know better."

"What exactly went down?" Tanasha inquired as she turned the car onto the west side highway heading downtown.

"A gang of niggas was waiting for us," Red spoke up, "but we got the drop on them first. It could've easily been you or Chandler who put them on about us coming!"

"Nigga, I been warning yo simple ass about my daddy for the longest. How you gon' even front like I would flip on you? That's fucked up Red! You know I love you!" Tears crested Tanasha's eyes.

"This shit smells sour all around, but Pops ain't been nothin' but good to me!" Red protested.

Decidedly, Heiress said "Tell him."

"Tell me what?" Red asked.

"When we get back to my spot," Tanasha replied.

"What spot? Yo, where the fuck are we going?"

Tanasha's spot was a loft she kept in lower Manhattan. It sat atop a modern building with all glass walls and windows. Due to its secretive purpose, it seemed ironic or so Red thought as they entered the large living space. Albeit sparsely furnished, it was tastefully decorated. An impressive collection of fine art gave it the feel of a contemporary wing in the Guggenheim. It surprised him that she had never brought him here - so much for love.

Tanasha's heels clicked loudly as she walked across the polished, marble floor. She briefly left the room, only to return and hand Red the red iPhone Chandler had given her earlier. He looked down at the screen to see a paused video. Pops was sitting in what appeared to be a hotel room.

"Play it," Tanasha directed. "It's the real thing."

Red's anger began to grow. Tanasha talking shit about her father was one thing, it was to be expected. Red thought she was spoiled and ill tempered. On the other hand, he knew Heiress to be about business and could be taken seriously.

He looked up from the phone without pressing play.

"What is this supposed to be?" He asked, stalling the inevitable. Heiress gritted her teeth as she looked down at the screen with him.

"Just watch it," she said without pity or remorse.

Red knitted his brows then walked toward the front area of the living room where he stood before a stretch of glass panes displaying a full view of downtown TriBeCa. He watched the recording, Black Pops with Mayor James calling for his head. What was worse, Black Pops appeared to be considering the offer. Red had to keep his hand from trembling; the sick thought of capping both Tanasha and Heiress to send Black Pops a message came and went.

He and Black Pops were close, at least that's what he thought. They had several conversations over the past few years where Black Pops actually discussed his brief foray into politics, as well as his disappointment with its inbuilt classism and racism. Red recalled a conversation where he had once told him

"He would hustle until he died, before ever walking down that road again." But the proof was in the pudding.

Red decided he needed to see Black Pops. This was possibly part of his plan. Perhaps, he let Pete's boys know he and Heiress were coming, knowing they would survive. In any event, he would have answers; and if he didn't like what he heard, he would put a slug in Black Pops' dome.

"Who gave you this?" Red called across the room to Tanasha who had retired to a white leather settee.

"Someone who knows what my daddy is really up to," she answered.

"It still doesn't make any sense," he turned as Heiress walked over to him. He passed her the phone then she viewed the video.

"If Mayor James is offering him some type of position, why wouldn't Pops just turn me over to him instead of having niggas trynna get me at the mortuary?"

"I can't make sense of the shit either," Heiress added. "But it still doesn't change the fact that he and Mayor James are fuck buddies, and them niggas want you dead."

"And what about you! What was all that shit you was talkin' at the meeting this morning?" He asked, walking over to Tanasha.

68

"I was just calling him on his shit!" She answered. "He front like he about to rid New York City of drugs and shit, when he really just taking niggas' territory for his own profit. He's lying to y'all; he built y'all up on some killing niggas for a good cause bullshit. You've been clearing the field for him.

The minute you find out what he's really up to, he knows there's a target on his ass." Standing, she joined Red and Heiress. "I ain't gotta lie to kick it. I want New Crop off the streets too. But weed, blow, mushrooms, and mollies - yeah a bitch wanna run that shit. There I said it, what!"

"But it don't stop there baby!" Tanasha continued, "I already told you my aunt Dolores put me on to him killing my momma. Guess who the nigga that got shot up with her was?"

"Tanasha!" Heiress cautioned, not certain Red should know after viewing the tape. Surely, he would wanna kill Pops but get himself killed in the process.

"No, fuck that! He needs to know! If I have to live with it, why shouldn't he!"

"Live with what?" Red inquired.

"He had your daddy killed too," Tanasha informed him. Red felt as though an electric charge had burned through his brain.

"That's right. Yo daddy was Killer Cartel just like my momma; and my daddy flipped on both of them the same way he's flippin' on us now. Ask Tammy! She knows the truth."

"Can I see you outside please?" Heiress asked while taking Red by the arm before he could say a word. She led him outside the loft onto a long, wrap around balcony into a cool, early evening breeze. Once alone, she turned to Red and said, "See what I mean. She wants too much for her own good and gon' wind up getting her ass killed. I know it's been years between you two but are you so invested that you're willing to stick around and try to save her?"

"How long have you known about my father?" Red asked.

"A while now. Tanasha put me on. So I did some digging around in the past myself. She wasn't lying. Looks like Pops had Cherish and your father murdered but the reason why is sketchy at best."

"I'm gonna kill him. I'ma kill him tonight Heiress."

"At this point, I think that's exactly what Tanasha wants, but you have to face the facts Red. Your dad was one of us. He knew what he was..."

"It doesn't matter!" Red declared. "When my father died, everything fell apart. Malcolm died, Tammy started hoeing, and my moms...my mom's died with her crack pipe. He did that to us!" Red gripped the balcony banister so tightly his knuckles were white.

"Leave it alone Red," Heiress warned. "I know you have enough loot to bounce. That's what the fuck I'm about to do. You should do the same."

"It ain't that easy and you know it. Pops ain't gon' just let us disappear. Naw, that nigga gotta die. Besides, I got some other shit to handle...I just can't up and leave." Red trailed off, perhaps realizing the enormity of what was occurring.

"What other shit?" Heiress asked. "That girl? I would leave her alone too Red before you get her hurt."

Red's heart seemed as if it had stopped. He knew she was talking about Aleide, but how did she know? Aleide, his Riverside Drive apartment, they were part of his life that was kept hidden from Killa Cartel. Unexpectedly, he felt his trigger finger begin to itch.

"What girl?" Was all he could muster. Heiress gave him a look that clearly said *nigga please*! then continued.

"Don't worry. I'm the only one who knows about her. I made sure of that."

"Tanasha?"

"Shorty would already be dead if Tanasha knew," Heiress said. "Nevertheless, I think it's time you let her go.
We can't care for people the way you care for her Red, not in this business. You know it could be used against you. Don't fool yourself Red. There are no happy endings for people like us, but she isn't like us. Leave her and disappear. Or stay and destroy her with your love."

"Easier said than done," Red confessed. He felt deflated; he realized Heiress was right. Oftentimes, he thought about just taking Aleide away from the states and disappearing. Up to this point, he had put away quite a substantial nest egg to live a fairly easy life. But what was life without Aleide? He would figure something out because he wouldn't leave her behind.

"How long have you known about us?" He whispered, quickly glancing back into the living room where Tanasha was occupied with reading a copy of the Daily News.

Heiress answered, "A little over a year. We crossed paths uptown on 125th. You didn't see me but I saw you. Your arm was wrapped around her; you were just-a-grinning. I was shocked. I had never seen you smile like that. Not for Tanasha, not for anybody. As a result, I followed you to your place on Riverside and watched you fuck her a couple of times.
You two have boring sex; it's not like when you're beatin' Tanasha. Anyway, I've been watching you two ever since. It's my thing."

"What the fuck Heiress! You a fucking stalker...and a pervert!" Red accused, embarrassed but a little turned on at the thought of her watching him fuck.

"Call it what you want. I was watching your back. I followed her when she was on her own also; I needed to be sure she was clean. I was careful and made sure no one else from Killa Cartel was onto you. How long do you think you can keep your little hideaway before Pops or Chandler finds out? You should be thanking me."

"Heiress," Red whispered her name, somewhat in awe. He never figured her for the guardian angel type.

"You know I'm right Red. Forget about getting back at Pops and get outta town. His time will come." Placing her hand atop his, they both looked on as dusk began to settle over the city. Somehow, Red knew it was going to be a busy night.

Chapter 8

Black Pops always wore black and was always sharp. He and Suga Momma stood before a triple paneled floor length mirror with her smoothing the lapels of his slick Armani tux, black shirt, and black bow tie. Suga was dressed to the nines as well, wearing a gauzy black, off the shoulder Dior gown encrusted with Swarovski crystals on the hem. Taking her out was a rare occasion. However, tonight they would be on the scene - rubbing shoulders with the city's elite at the Mayor's annual gala for the arts. Looking into the eyes of the man she adored, Suga Momma couldn't have been happier when she heard: "Bitch, could you stop fucking with my muthafucking coat so we can get the fuck outta here?"

"I just wanted to make sure you was looking good daddy," spat Suga, "You non-appreciating muthafucka. You ain't never got nothing good to say. I don't even know why I'm with yo ass!" She cursed.

"The car is here sir," announced a squat blond girl, in a maid's uniform with a Russian accent.

"Thank you Elka," Black Pops responded. To Suga Momma he snapped, "You wanna go to this shit or sit here and argue all night!?"

"Fuck you nigga! You know I wanna go so why you asking?" Suga countered, pushing pass him and storming out of the room. Black Pops smirked, caught up with her, and then delivered a hard slap to her left buttock.

"Stop!" She said laughing, scurrying away as he gave chase.

The two entered the private elevator that served as an entrance to his three floor townhouse on Manhattan's Upper West Side and exited into a grand lobby of granite walls and sparkling chandeliers. Chandler stood next to a black stretch limo that was awaiting them out front; he pulled Black Pops aside.

"Any updates?" Asked Black Pops.

"As of yet, no one's heard from Red or Heiress. And Ross's folks knew I was coming from a mile away; I couldn't get close to them."

"It's because I've had you outta the field too long," said Black Pops. "Being head of my security and taking out a heavily guarded target are two different elements.
I should've sent Red instead," he mused, burning Chandler with his words.

"Well, as of now, Red is off the radar. I can only assume he suspects you set him up to die."

"Get Ivy and Deel to find him before the night is out. Put a team out to get eyes on Heiress as well," Black Pops commanded. Then he added, "You don't think...it couldn't have been Tanasha, could it?"

"I don't think she would go as far as to turn on her own peoples Pops," answered Chandler. "But she is a little power hungry," he admitted.

"Find them and bring them to me," Pops said while getting into the limo.

"Will do," smiled Chandler. As the car drove off, he pulled out his phone and dialed. Seconds later, Tanasha's voice buzzed into his ear.

"They left separately about half an hour ago. I hope you have eyes on them."

"I do. I have Ivy and Deel tracking Red , but the twins have lost Heiress. And you?"

"I'm on my way to meet him now," Tanasha stated.

"Good. Be careful baby," Chandler said warmly.

"Don't worry baby. I can handle Lil Reggie. He wants this just as much as we do. With his big brother out-of-the-way, the only two people between us and the keys to the empire is my daddy and Lil Reggie's mama.

Shirley Mitgowen was a harsh, frail woman who had somehow survived well pass her due date. Rail thin and wrinkled like a prune, her golden pallor and coif of manicured silver hair spoke of wealth, in the new money sense, in spite of her drained appearance. She had been ranting all day about the death of her baby and grand baby, and how her good-for-nothing surviving son was doing nothing about it. Big Ross's younger brother, Lil Reggie was anything but what his name implied. At six foot five and 320 pounds, he was quite an imposing figure, but none of that mattered to Ms. Shirley.

Surrounded by no less than ten armed men, they stood in a Victorian style reception room which was carved out of expensive, dark walnut, and filled with heavy wooden furniture.

"Why haven't you found out who killed my babies!" She raged. "What in the hell good are you if you gon' just stand around looking like a bunch of faggots! Y'all ain't shit, as long as the muthafuckas that did this is still alive! Reggie! REGGIE! You hear me boy!"

"Dang! I already told you I'm taking care of it momma!" Lil Reggie answered.

"Don't you curse me boy!" Screamed the woman as though he had mugged her. "Ross wouldn't have ever cursed at me like that, you disrespectful muthafucka!" She cried, jumping up and slapping him on the jaw with as much power as she could muster - it wasn't much.

Lil Reggie stomped out of the room and made a call on his cell phone.

"Hello!" Tanasha's voice came across the receiver.

"Yo! Could you hurry up and get over here to kill this bitch!" He spat, exacerbated.

"I'm on my way baby," was Tanasha's response. "I can't wait to see you again," she added, becoming moist.

"Just get here," he countered. "The sooner this bitch is dead, the sooner we can move on with our plans. You still want me don't you baby?" He cooed.

"Baby, I want it all," replied Tanasha.

Chapter 9

For Aleide, there was no other feeling like it in the world when Red's tongue was inside her. She grabbed the back of his head and stroked his soft, coppery curls as she trust her hips to match the rhythm of his movements. In the past, Red had never been as generously oral with others as he was with Aleide. In truth, he was accustomed to chicks being blown away by his dick size, and having his way as a result. Eating pussy was barely an afterthought. But for Aleide, he would suck on her lips and make her gush all day. He slowly traced the outside of her clit with the very tip of his tongue, sending waves of pleasure through her body directly down to her toes.

He kissed and French kissed her lower lips like he was kissing her mouth, darting his tongue in and out of her in quick, successive strokes. Aleide squirmed and wiggled while making little bird like chirps to keep from screaming. She had learned a lot from Red - how to dress sexier, what type of underwear to wear, as well as how to wax her pussy clean.

His entire mouth was covering her now, sucking her lips into his mouth while burying his tongue deep inside her. Aleide couldn't take it anymore; she let off a high-pitch squeal that she muffled by covering her mouth with both hands. Red pulled his tongue out and rested its tip on the hood of her clit, sending her squirting into overdrive.

"Oh god! Fuck...I want you in me baby," she begged, staring down into his eyes. Red mounted up and grabbed her by her hips. Aleide reached down and began rubbing the apple-sized head against her dripping pussy lips. Licking her teeth with a pointed tongue, she looked up into his eyes then closed them as he entered her. The feeling of her tight canal slowly enveloping his dick combined with the taste of her in his mouth melted away the uncertainty of tomorrow. He loved her; he rarely said it aloud but today he did.

Red pushed her onto her back, she wrapped her legs around his waist, tensing, bracing herself for his full length. He put it down, feeling her open up the deeper he pushed. Aleide yelped as he buried himself to the hilt. He remained there, grinding in a slow, circular motion, causing them both to shudder in ecstasy.

Red wrapped his arms around her waist and cupped her ass cheeks with his hands while continuing to grind deeply into her. He pulled her closer, so much so that they could feel each other's hearts beating against the other; then he whispered, "I love you baby," into her ear. Tears fell from Aleide's eyes. Lost in the pleasure of his thrusts, she sensed something was wrong. Even so, her only response was, "I love you too Jamarcus," she then softly kissed his face all over.

Suddenly, he stood up, lifting Aleide with him and began pounding into her, bouncing her petite frame up and down on his long pipe. Aleide emitted little cries of pleasure as well as pain, grabbed him by the back of his head, forcing her tongue into his mouth. He pulled away, leaned down, taking one of her coin-sized nipples into his mouth sucking, and then biting ever so softly. She flooded him. A gush of clear juice sprayed from her as he continued to lift her up and down on his dick as though she were a barbell. Her wetness traveled and oozed down his shaft wetting the floor which caused him to release. Red came up off her nipple and gasped out loud. Throwing her back onto the bed with her legs spread wide, he pounded his nut into her.

Aledie's head rolled from side-to-side as she felt him swell with each thrust. When he finally collapsed atop her covered in perspiration and breathing heavily, she stroked his forehead lovingly. "I love you too," she whispered.

They lay silent in each other's arms for nearly twenty minutes when Aleide announced she was hungry. Therefore, they showered and dressed, and decided they would grab a couple of slices of pizza up on Broadway. Red knew something was up the second they left his apartment. He didn't have any physical evidence to draw on but somehow he knew he had been made.

He took Aleide by the hand and led her quickly up the block while trying to appear normal.

"Slow down Jamarcus, I'm wearing heels," she complained.

"My bad. I'm just mad hungry," he apologized, looking around cautiously. Typically, he was so much more calm and collected in a potentially hazardous situation. Then again, he never had Aleide's personal safety as a concern either.

He thought perhaps they should double back to his apartment and hole up there, but then he knew that would cause her to become alarmed and ask questions he wasn't prepared to answer.

"Hey. Are you ok? You seem distracted," Aleide stopped walking but held his hand tightly. Red paused for a moment, seemingly at a loss for words. Then he stated, "It's my job. They fucking want to transfer me to one of their international offices. It's a big ass raise, and I'll have to talk white all the time, but...I didn't know how to tell you. I didn't know if I accepted the position if you would come with me."

"So...can you say no?" Asked Aleide, somewhat relieved the source of her worry was a simple work issue.

"Kinda not, if I wanna stay in my profession," lied Red. "The New York branch is being absorbed."

"I would love to go Jamarcus. It's just that I can't imagine leaving momma all alone, but..."

"She can come too baby. We together right?" He lifted her chin so that their eyes met. "You do love me, don't you baby?"

"Of course Jamarcus. I'd follow you to the ends of the earth," Aleide affirmed. "I think it's great they want to promote you...yes! I'm sure my moms...with some working on would be open to it," she smiled reassuringly. "Yes...but where are they transferring you to?"

Red hadn't thought of that yet. Luckily, he was quick on his feet. "Uh, um, Germany," he stammered then repeated it again confidently.

"Whoa, Europe's strongest economy," Aleide smiled.

"Is it?" Red asked offhandedly.

"Of course it is. You know that silly, you're an accountant." She gave his hand a squeeze then emitted a relaxed sigh. "Wow! Germany...just like that huh?"

"Just like that," Red agreed, then stated, "Yo, let's grab some real Italian instead of dollar slices. There's that joint we always pass down on 90th Street."

"Let's," Aleide agreed with stars in her eyes. She thought a sudden move to Germany might be just what she needed to shake up the mundane. She was born and raised in Harlem and could definitely use a break from New York City.

In the end, she wanted to one day become his wife and mother to his children. Germany would be as good a place as any to lay down that foundation.

They ate at Luigi's, a small hole in the wall that offered a cozy atmosphere, great food, and excellent wine. Aleide was picking at the remnants of her penne Bolognese while gazing lovingly into his eyes.
Red, on the other hand, seemed preoccupied. His eyes darted about the restaurant in occasional intervals as though he was looking for parking on a crowded strip.

"Are you worried about leaving?" She asked soothingly.

"No, it's not that. This shit just sprung up on us today. Guess I would miss New York," he sighed and looked up at the ceiling.

"What about your apartment; would you sale,... sublet?"

"Neither"," he said. "I mean I own the spot; I'm not strapped for cash..." His voice trailed off as he cautiously watched a group of youth pass the eatery's large front window.

"I didn't know you owned it," said Aleide. "Why didn't I ever know that? What else you been hiding from me?"

"I never told you?" Asked Red, and after some consideration, he answered, "It was willed to me."

"Someone in your family handed it down to you?"

"No...no," he responded. Lost in thought for a moment, he paused then smiled at the memory playing through his mind.

He held precious few warm memories and realized at that moment, other than his love for Aleide, he had shared even less.

"When I was sixteen," he began, "I ran into this old Jewish lady, Mrs. Pritchett; she was a widow who lived by herself. Anyway, it was pouring that day, I had just finished a job...um was on my way home from work," he corrected. "Well, she was a mess, soaked to her bones and looking lost. No one was attempting to help her. So I walked over to her and offered my assistance. Turns out, she was almost blind and had wondered away from her crib the night before. Everyone just assumed she was homeless.

Dirty Red: A Killa's Love Story

I walked her home, got her inside into some dry clothes, and spoon fed her a can of chunky soup," he chuckled lightly. "Afterwards, we sat and drank spice tea while she told me mad stories about her youth. You know how old people like to talk, but I was with it...it was an escape."

"After that night, I made sure to stop by a couple of times a week, to make sure she was eating, keep her company, run errands, shit like that."

Aleide's eyes became wide and filled with love. "Oh my god baby, you never told me you did something like that for someone. You're amazing!"
Red smiled but shifted uncomfortably. "Yeah, I did that for a couple of years. Then one day I stopped by to see her and the super told me she had passed. He was happy to see me though. Ol' girl had left me everything - the apartment and all her belongings. That's why all the furniture is antique."

Realization blossomed across Aleide's face, "So that explains the old black and white photos of white people hung up in the hallway, and the one of the old lady on your living room mantel. I just thought you were being hipster," she laughed.

89

Red laughed too. For him, old lady Pritchett was therapy of sorts. Becoming a hired gun at such a young age, he needed someone or something to take care of similar to the way a shut in needs a goldfish for company. Old lady Pritchett was his goldfish. Caring for her kept him connected to what small measure of humanity he had left in what he considered a demonic heart. He believed he was a demon of death regardless of all the good Black Pops told him he was doing for the streets.

He and Aleide walked down Broadway arm-in-arm. She leaned her head on his strong shoulder, and felt closer and more in love with him than she ever had before.
Regardless of the cloud of death that hung over him, he too believed their future was bright. It was early evening, just after 7:00 p.m. Streets were bustling with the activity of shoppers as well as individuals who were just out and about. *"We will have our tomorrow,"* thought Red but the resolution was short-lived. He noticed a quick reflection behind him in the window of a passing cab and realized the separate lives he had lead up to that point only had precious seconds before they collided.

Alarmed, Red turned around, briefly catching sight of Ivy, another one of Black Pops' wet men. Red searched with his eyes but the man had already disappeared. He took Aleide's hand and began dragging her with him, "We've gotta get off the street," he said with calm determination.

"He saw us," Ivy whispered under his breath, "cut them off at the corner." The wisp of a man was merely five foot five and as thin as a crack head on holiday. A cuddly mix of Gary Coleman and a grasshopper, he didn't have much in the way of appearance either.

"What the hell Jamarcus, slow down!" Aleide cried while trying to pull away, but Red held firmly to her wrist. There were a thousand thoughts racing through his mind.

Ahead of them, at the end of the block, a thickset, six foot package of solid black muscle barred their way. The bald man with unnaturally grey eyes extended a flat palm cautioning them to stop.

"Shit! Deel!" Red pushed Aleide aside while continuing to charge forward. He dropped low, but Deel saw the sweep coming and jumped back several feet.

Red anticipated the move, scrambled forward into a rolling flip, catching Deel just under the chin with the flat of his foot. Deel cursed as he bit down on his tongue, filling his mouth with blood and saliva. He stumbled backwards, throwing several unsuccessful blows at Red's head. Red was swift and stealthy in his movements; he cleared the man's massive arms, getting in close enough to head-butt him.

Deel fell backwards from the dizzying blow, then immediately felt the burning sensation of a bullet tear into his throat. Next, another one entered his forehead. Deel's body hit the ground with a loud thump followed by a blood curdling scream from Aleide. Red turned around to find Ivy with his forearm around her neck and a 9 millimeter pressed against the side of her head. Red didn't hesitate to shoot, shattering the wrist of the deathly thin man's gun hand.

He rushed forward, cracking Ivy over the eye with the butt of his PPK, grabbed Aleide, and pulled her into traffic in order to cross over to the west side of 102nd.

Aleide screamed again, as another assailant scurried over a cab with his weapon drawn.

"Who the fuck!" cursed Red. He flung Aleide against the cab while simultaneously releasing a thin razor shank hidden in his cuff. He waved his hands wildly, dipped behind and brought the blade to the man's neck, slashing until several thin slices in his Adam's apple became an open shower of blood, drenching Aleide and the side of the cab. She screamed in terror, kicked off her heels, and ran for dear life through a torrent of oncoming cars. Never had she experienced such violence. She had no idea what was going on. What was worse was she had no idea who her man was. He appeared to be in his element, completely at home with the brutality he was administering.

Red caught up with her three blocks up at 106th and forcefully pulled her off the busy street into a deserted alleyway.

"Let me go! Get away from me," Aleide swatted at him crying hysterically. Red wasn't listening though; he was on high alert. It wasn't until she dug her nails deep into his forearm that she got his attention, at which point he stopped dragging but then flung her to the ground.

"Shut the fuck up and keep yo ass right there!" He whispered harshly, sending new waves of fear to the blood-soaked girl. Aleide was so scared she thought she might piss herself. For that reason, she did as she was told. After several minutes of waiting, Red reached down and offered his hand. She was quick to slap it away.

"Don't touch me!" She yelled. "I can stand by myself."

"We have to get you home," he said. "It's too dangerous to take you back to my..."

"Who are you!?" Shrieked Aleide. "Who were those men? Why do you know how to fight like that?"

"Aleide, I can explain everything but I'ma need you to calm down."

"Calm down, Jamarcus! You just slit a man's throat and covered me in his blood goddamit! My man the fucking accountant! I knew this shit was too good to be true!
You shot a man...you shot them," she wailed. Red reached for her only to have his hand slapped away yet again.

"Don't! Fucking! Touch! Me!" Aleide was trembling not only from fear but the coolness of the wet blood plastered all over her.

"Baby, don't say that," Red's voice cracked ever so slightly. "I know this shit is crazy but..."

"You lied to me! Didn't you?" Aleide demanded. She was putting two and two together and beginning to see the bigger picture.

"You're not an accountant are you? You're not being transferred to Germany either are you?

You're in trouble and you're running. Am I right Jamarcus? What did you do?" She asked, now sobbing, "You've done something bad haven't you? And people want you dead. Don't lie to me Jamarcus, I swear to God. Damn you! Don't lie to me anymore."

"Baby, just let me explain..."

"Explain what? I have five brothers Jamarcus! Two dead! Two on Rikers, and one on work release. Do you know what they all have in common? Breaking women's hearts while explaining their bullshit crimes! And you're just like them! A fucking lying, drug dealing, car stealing nigga!"

"You don't know what the fuck you're talking about Aleide. If you would just let a nigga talk!" Red said trying to get a word in. But Aleide wasn't having it. "You're absolutely right! I don't know you do I? I don't know who the fuck you are; so tell me! Is your name even Jamarcus Stacy?"

"Stop being like that baby. I never meant to hurt you or have shit go down like this. I'm sorry baby, but I'm gon' fix this shit, ok. I'm sorry!"

"Sorry for what Jamarcus?"

"For not telling you from the jump what I really do for a living."

"And what's that?" Aleide was at a lost.

"I'm a contract killer."

"Fuck me..." gasped Aleide.

Chapter 10

Big Ross Mitgowen's family home was located on a secluded block in Harlem's historical Hamilton Heights neighborhood just off 147th Street. The elegant, four story Brownstone was built in the late 19th century and covered considerable grounds for a New York City residence. With Culture Club's "Karma Chameleon" pumping through her ear buds, Tanasha Black easily found her way into the magnificent home. Its security system had been compromised by one of its inhabitants.

Tanasha seemed to be moving in slow motion as she turned down a lit corridor guarded by several armed men, and tossed two small metal canisters onto the floor. Big Ross's men jumped back in shock at the sudden appearance of the masked buxom goddess of death, dressed in black boots, gloves, goggles, and a leather bodysuit. She couldn't hear their warnings as they scrambled away from the choking release of teargas filling the cramped space, and rushed forward.

In her hands she held small, cylindrical devices resembling fountain pens and unleashed streams of searing sulfuric acid.

The men recoiled back in pain, screaming as the clear liquid burned through cloth and flesh like hot piss melting snow. Tanasha walked pass the men writhing on the floor then tossed a small explosive over her shoulder. Seconds later, an explosion rocked the second floor as she calmly made her way up the stairwell to the third story. On the upper floors, Ross's men went into defense/panic mode.

His widow, Dorothea had collapsed in the corner wailing, holding her cross close to her chest as her mother-in-law, Ms. Shirley berated her for cowardice.

Tanasha came out of the stairwell and was face-to-face with an AR-15 toting man. Without delay, she doused his grill with a shot of acid, causing him to drop the gun and grab at his already dissolving nose and eyes. Tanasha ignored the gun and rushed ahead; she ran up on another guard, stabbing him several times in the neck with a small, sharp blade. She caught another man in the throat with the same blade, flinging it down the length of the corridor as he attempted to get off a shot.

"Come with me momma! We have to get outta here!" Urged Lil Reggie, taking the old woman by the hand.

"I'm not running anywhere!" protested Ms. Shirley, pulling free. "This shit would've never happened if my Ross was here. Ain't nobody ever dared!" She wept. The words stung Lil Reggie all the more. She always favored Ross over him in any given situation. Even in his death, she favored him. He thought, *"don't worry bitch. You 'bout to join that nigga!"*

"Surround us!" He called out to the five armed men in the room. "We have to get my momma downstairs to safety!"

"The whole shit on fire down there! This is a fortified room. It'll buy us some time while we take the fire escape down," one of the men declared. Yet, Lil Reggie insisted on leaving. Not only did he need his mother out of the secure room to place her in Tanasha's path, it was also important that several of his men witnessed it.

"I'm staying right here ya hear me!" Said Ms. Shirley. *"There's no way T's getting through that door,"* thought Lil Reggie. Just then a blast rocked them from above.

"They're on the roof too!" Lil Reggie cried then charged for the door. Behind him, he heard Dorothea scream out, and turned to see one side of her face melting like an ice cream cone left out in the sun. Tanasha used the blast on the roof as a diversion then came through the window instead with the help of a second grenade.

Ms. Shirley croaked out a shrill whimper as Tanasha pumped nine slugs into her chest and face. The guards, stunned from the double explosions, were slow to respond. They were frozen with fear and rage as the old woman's body hit the hardwood floor.

"Momma!" Lil Reggie wailed in feigned agony then felt himself slammed against the door as Tanasha put a slug in his shoulder and thigh for good measure. Just as quickly as she had come, she had disappeared. The two surviving guards helped him to his feet and over to his mother's dead body. Even through the pain of being shot, he had to suppress a smile. Tanasha had kept her end of the bargain.

An army of police sirens could be heard in the background. A crowd had already gathered outside the burning Brownstone. Tanasha calmly walked through the throng of people as though she was also a spectator. Inside, Lil Reggie's men had to drag him from his mother's corpse over to the fire escape. He was happy to see Ross's home burn down and her with it. Now it was all his.

"I didn't sign up for this shit Jamarcus," Aleide said. She sat next to Red in a yellow cab, arms crossed over her chest to hide as much of her bloodstained shirt as possible.

"I know," said Red.

"Now what?" She whimpered. "What are you gonna to do with me?"

"Take you someplace safe where you can get cleaned up then get you home to yo ma."

"How do I know these people don't know where I live?" Her eyes were filled with fear and anger. Red thought about Heiress and wondered if she was truly the only one who knew about Aleide.

"You and yo moms can't stay there for long. Like I said, we gotta bounce."

101

"I'm not going anywhere with you," Aleide spat the words out with a trembling voice. "For all I know, you killed that baby yesterday!"

Her words were like a rusty blade twisting in his heart. Maybe he was being naive in thinking they could stay together now that she was aware he was a paid assassin. Confirming his hand in Tamar Mitgowen's death would be the end of their relationship for certain. He decided then and there, he would take that to the grave.

The cab pulled up at the corner of 121st and Lex, the two hopped out, quickly paying the driver, and making off like fugitives on the run. They hurried two blocks up to 123rd and made their way to a closed, 99¢ store storefront. They walked down the steps to the basement level, Red knocked a couple of times on the window.

The door of the store opened to the accompaniment of jiggling bells. A thick, chinky-eyed, light-skinned chick in black lace and a red feather boa answered the door.

"Boy, I was thinking you wasn't coming! Get in here," she said, ushering Red and Aleide through the door.

"Good looking Kat," Red gave the woman a kiss on the cheek. "Yo, this is Aleide. Aleide, Kat."

"Charmed." Kat held out her hand, giving the blood soaked Aleide a thorough once over.

"What the fuck you don' did to this girl Red?"

"I told you on the phone some niggas ran up on us. Can you get her cleaned up?"

"Yeah. Let's get y'all downstairs." Kat began making her way toward the back of the store. Red and Aleide followed.

"What is this place?" Aleide whispered to Red.

"See for yourself," answered Kat. Then she opened a door for them to step through. They entered a backroom filled with stock for the storefront and navigated to a far corner where a hidden enclave revealed a downward staircase. Kat took the lead with Aleide sandwiched between herself and Red.

The stairwell opened onto a pink lounge area where several women, similarly dressed in garters and lingerie, lounged about on a red sectional watching R&B Divas on a large wall-mounted flat screen. Everyone perked up when Red entered the room, lavishing him with seductive hellos, gestures, and winks.

"Alright hoes put ya pussy back in they traps, he got his bitch with him." Kat proclaimed as she escorted them through the room. Aleide self-consciously covered herself barely aware of the insulting reference.

They followed Kat down a long, door-lined hallway which was akin to a hotel, complete with the obvious sounds of fucking emitting from many of them. Red felt embarrassed for Aleide, even more that she would have to lay low in a brothel for the time being.

Kat showed them to a room, pink like the hallway, with a pink rug, heart shaped bed, and flat screen T.V. showing a black on white cheerleader gangbang already in progress. She gave Aleide a smile. "Make yourself comfortable. You can shower in there. I'll get you some fresh clothes. Would you prefer a nurse's uniform or lace?" She asked snidely.

"Yo cut the shit Kat!" Red ordered. "Where's Tammy?"

"She's at some art function shit," whined Kat. "Black Pops had her bring a few of the white girls to work the crowd."

"Black Pops is there? At a black tie event?" Asked Red.

"Something like that," Kat responded, growing apprehensive. She had been working under Red's sister, Tamia for close to a decade now, and was one of the working girls in the establishment who knew what Red really did. The other girls simply thought he was some young baller with dough.

"I'ma need a tux," he said, removing his gat and placing it on the bed along with two extra clips.

"I'll see if we have anything in your size in our role playing wardrobe," Kat replied.

Once she was out of the room Aleide went berserk.

"A pimp! You're a pimp too?"

"My sister Tammy runs this place. Been doing so for about 15 years; it's called the Northern Tip."

"Fitting," snapped Aleide, removing her blood stained clothes and tossing them to the floor. "This is so retarded. I'm not staying here and you're not leaving me! AND WHO THE FUCK IS BLACK POPS!?"

"I have some business to handle. This is the safest place for you to stay. Even if Pops sent niggas out, the bitches here are loyal to Tammy first. They won't snitch you out."

"Oh my god! Snitching! Jamarcus!" Aleide covered her mouth and fresh tears began to fall.

"Wash up. Get dressed and wait for me. I'll come back for you Aleide. I promise."

"You'd better you motherfucker," she sobbed then collapsed into his arms. Red kissed her, snaking his tongue into her mouth while slipping a finger into her moist pussy. He could feel himself begin to grow and pushed his finger deeper inside her then…"NO!" Shouted Aleide, pushing him away from her. Breathing heavily, she fell to the bed and curled into the fetal position. Her mess of matted, dark hair covered her face.

"Leave me alone; go do what you have to do," she muttered bitterly.

Chapter 11

Red arrived at Lincoln Center at a quarter past nine wearing a black and white penguin tux. He was immediately denied entrance into the Mayor's gala event. However, Red was insistent.

"I can assure you I am a member of Mr. Lucas's private security," he said. "He's inside."

"Sir, once again, I can't let you in without an invite," the guard repeated. At that exact moment, he was interrupted by a voice cracking across his radio telling him to let Red through. Red smiled, satisfied he had gotten pass his first barrier, but anxious because someone knew he was coming.

"You clean up nice. Are you armed?" Chandler seemed to appear out of nowhere and took Red by the arm. "Where's your top hat? You look like the fucking Monopoly man," he quipped.

"You're here too," said Red, "How's Deel? How's his head?"

"Killing Deel - not a good move," Chandler counseled. "Pops ain't happy about that shit." He patted Red down then checked his coat.

"You think I give a fuck if he's pissed? I left the toy at home, now take me to him."

"He's busy right now," Chandler informed him. "But I'd like to talk with you for a minute." Chandler escorted Red to a private, windowless room somewhere in the bowels of Lincoln Center. It resembled an interrogation room. Inside its white walled interior were two black folding chairs with a metal framed Formica table between them.

Chandler was first to take a seat and crossed his hands over a folded leg. He seemed to be waiting for Red to either sit or speak. Red sat across from him, looking him in the eyes.

"Did you make the call to Pretty Piper warning him about me and Heiress?"

"I believe my target received a similar call," was Chandler's answer. "Their security was crazy deep. But I didn't disappear after having yet another public shootout."

"That wasn't a no," said Red.

"Not a yes either, but we have greater concerns. That's why you're here right?" Chandler inquired.

"It turns out Pops isn't the man we both thought he was. In fact, he's been playing us for years now.

I didn't want to believe it myself, but after finding out he's setting up new heads to distribute New Crop..."

"He and the mayor," Red interjected.

"How do you know about that?" Asked Chandler.

"A little birdy whispered in my ear," Red answered. "I need to see Pops...now. I don't give a fuck if he's becoming a kingpin or not. I have some other shit to discuss with him that ain't got shit to do with New Crop!"

"Like your father?" Asked Chandler.

"You know too? Then you know why I'm here," Red announced, beginning to rise from his seat.

"Relax Red. I'm not here to stop you," he assured by pulling out a silver Glock 23 then sliding it across the table. "I think you gon' need some help."

"What do you get out of me taking out Pops?" Asked Red suspiciously.

"A target off my back. Like I said, the Mitgowens were waiting for me today too. It seems I'm just as expendable as you. Therefore, I'll be leaving with a considerable amount of his cash."

"Classy move - his head of security cutting and running," Red jabbed with sarcasm.

"I never claimed there was honor among thieves," Chandler stood. "I'll be going now," he said then headed toward the door.

"Wait!" Red called out. "Why didn't you do it?" He asked.

"It somehow seems better coming from you." Chandler answered with a smile, then said "follow the sound of music and clink of Champagne glasses." He exited the room, leaving Red alone.

Red navigated through the crowd of fancy dressed patrons in the main ballroom of the art gala, but had yet to find Black Pops. A group had formed in a far corner of the room where several reporters were jockeying for space. In the middle of all the fuss was Mayor James engaged in a fiery impromptu debate with Luca De Ha Miller, a frog princess in a white, crystal encrusted gown. As Red moved in, he caught Black Pops standing to the Mayor's left. He had a mind to kill him on the spot, but determined he wanted Black Pops to know it was him rather than deliver an anonymous slug to the dome.

"What are you doing here?" Red felt a soft hand wrap around his arm and turned to be face-to-face with Tammy.

She wore a skintight, floor length gown of ruby sequins. Her ample cleavage was tastefully displayed, and her immaculate copper waves flowed down the length of her back. She was a beautiful woman indeed, bright and freckled like Red, with large almond shaped eyes and endless jet lashes.

"Did you know he killed our father?" Red inquired accusingly.

"Don't be stupid," Tammy warned. "Where are you getting your information?" She asked. Red saw that Black Pops had noticed them.

"I was told you knew the truth about it," he continued.

"I'm more interested in the girl you're hiding out at my establishment. Who is she?"

"My lady; I'm protecting her from him."

"And why haven't I met her?"

"You know why Tammy. I don't want her to have anything to do with this world."

"How's that working out for you?" Tammy remarked then stated, "Let's go. He's calling us."

Tammy led Red through the crowd of socialites, smiling and acknowledging several clients along the way. They exited the ballroom and made their way down several polished corridors until they reached a large mahogany door with a brass knob. Red opened the door allowing Tammy to step through first, then followed. He was greeted by the sight of Black Pops, propped behind a large mahogany desk with his feet kicked up.

"The prodigal fucking son returns!" He announced, flicking ashes from his cigar onto the floor. "Boy! What the fuck got into you today?" He sat up and placed his elbows on the desk. Present in the room were him, Black Pops, and Tammy. However, Red knew Pops had to have a shooter hidden somewhere in the cut.

"It was a simple job Red. Instead, I get two days of sloppy shit. What the fuck's been going on with you boy? And where the hell is Heiress?" Asked Black Pops who was a tad too jovial for Red.

"Shit got real today," Red retorted. "Mad muthafuckas was waiting for me and Heiress when we hit uptown! Heiress, being the chick she is, decided to lay low until we know what's up."

Red's delivery was cool and collected with no trace of emotion. Black Pops frowned, shaking his head sadly, offended at the suggestion he sent them on a death mission.

"Boy, who been filling yo head with this mess? Huh? I mean what you come down here to do Red? Fuck me up? Nigga you work for me. You on my muthafucking clock right now, and I get a call you uptown popping off my niggas running around with a Chinese bitch!"

Red could've laughed at that one but kept a straight face. How am I supposed to explain to Deel's people one of my own killed one of my own?" Asked Black Pops.

"Hopefully, as good as you can explain to me why you and Mayor James plotting against a nigga! Yeah, I know what's up," Red informed him. He pulled out the silver Glock 23 and took aim at Black Pops, who sat still, calmly watching.

"The fact that you haven't shot me means you might be willing to listen to reason son," said black Pops with faux applause. Red kept the Glock trained on the man who had taken him and Tammy in as children when they had no one to turn to. He molded them into two distinct roles, Red a killer and Tammy a madam.

"What are you doing Red?" Asked Tammy; she sashayed over to the desk and sat on its edge. "Put that thing away before you get yourself killed." She was both soft-spoken and sarcastic, as was her way.
Red's grip tightened on the weapon. Would she have told Black Pops about Aleide at the Northern Tip? Red wasn't certain, Black Pops and Tammy looked mighty cozy together.

"You don't understand Tammy! Black Pops rolled on me to the muthafucking Mayor! I saw them niggas talking about it last night!" He continued, not lowering his weapon. Black Pops sat up a little straighter at the mention of his clandestine meeting with the Mayor. Tammy looked only mildly interested.

"Nigga, you been following me?" Black Pops asked, smiling as he always did. Red never did like that about him; he could never really tell if the man was genuinely pissed off or not.

"You also killed our father," Red accused venomously.

"I killed yawl's daddy!" Black Pops laughed. "Lawd have mercy please! Tammy, what is this nigga talking about?" Black Pops tapped Tammy on the ass further angering Red.

"Somebody's playing with your head little brother. Care to share who?" Tammy removed a Virginia Slim from a thin gold case and placed it between her lips. She leaned over toward Black Pops; he lit it with a platinum lighter.

"He ain't denying the shit though! Is he?" Red snarled.

"Now what Red, you gon' put a hole in my head? Tammy! Tell yo little brother how much I hate it when a nigga aims a gun at me."

Tammy rolled her eyes. "Especially from a nigga I taught everything he know," continued Black Pops.

"Nigga, if I wanted to turn you over to Randy James, you wouldn't be standing here right now. I got Chandler looking into what went down over at Sam's, but that don't give you no cause to walk up in this bitch like you that nigga! I'm that muthafucking nigga!" Black Pops rose to his feet, slamming an open palm against the desktop.

"Fuck you and that cracker-ass muthafucka!" Red shouted. "This about you killing my pops and destroying my family!"

"Nigga, I'm the one that kept together what little bit of family you had left!" Black Pops struck the table again.
"Now I don't know who the fuck been filling yo head with this bullshit young nigga but you best get that gun outta my face!"

"Tammy, why you co-signing this nigga?" Spat Red. Tammy took a pull from her cigarette and blew the smoke in the air.

"Because you're wrong," she said matter-of-factly.

"This is bullshit. I saw the tape of you and Mayor James with my own eyes..." began Red, but Black Pops was quick to cut him off.

"Fuck Randy! This ain't got shit to do with his bitch ass. This about your lack of trust and loyalty!"

"Loyalty!" Shouted Red. "You kicking it with the enemy talking about getting a council seat in exchange for my head! What the nigga say? He gon' cut my tongue out so I can't talk!"

"Tammy, will you talk some sense into this young nigga," Black Pops requested, stroking her exposed back.

"Be smart Red," Tammy stood and walked over to him, but he kept the gun aimed in Black Pops direction. "Randolph James ain't nothing but a tool baby," she continued. "And he has a purpose. Just like you, just like me. Pops didn't have shit to do with daddy's death.
So why don't you stay in your lane," she slowly pushed his hand down lowering the gun.

"*What the fuck is going on between you two?*" Red wondered, looking back and forth between her and Black Pops. Tammy's hand was still on the barrel of the Glock, which was now pointing toward the floor.

"Stay alive and find out nigga," said Black Pops; he wasn't smiling. "I swear to god Red if I didn't need yo ass alive," he said. "Major worked for me.

He was a good wet man, almost as good as you. I loved yo daddy like he was my own blood Red. Two times that nigga saved my life. I had his muthafucking back the same way I always had yours. Cherish killed yo daddy, tell him Tammy; she was there."

"Tanasha's mother!" Red declared with alarm.

"It's true Red," said Tammy with a bit more sympathy than she had previously shown.

"Major found out Cherish was working to unseat me as head of Killa Cartel. She tried to get him to link up with her, but yo daddy was a loyal nigga and let me know what was up. When I confronted Cherish, she denied everything and tried to cap me all in one breath. If Major hadn't jumped in front of me, I would've been a dead muthafucka. She got away and went off the grid. About two weeks later, she and her niggas lit my man up right in front of Tammy and yo momma. I vowed to find the bitch and get her back for what she did, and I did. I couldn't stop Gladys from losing herself in that pipe, but I made sure you and yo sister was taken care of," Pops revealed, easing back down into his seat.

Red was speechless. He wondered if Tanasha knew the whole time. Had she been playing him just to get him to take out Black Pops? But why not just do it herself? And how did Ivy and Deel know where to find him? He naturally assumed they were out to wet him, but when did they start tailing him?

Red pondered it and decided they must have been on him since he left Tanasha's crib. She was the only one who could have informed them he was with her at the time. The thought of Tanasha betraying him burned him to his core. True, he loved Aleide but he and Tanasha had history together.

Red looked at the gun in his hand and thought about the man who gave it to him, Chandler Saint Jean. It was then he resolved Chandler and Tanasha must be working together, as impossible as it sounded in his mind. Suddenly, he felt a tinge of remorseful humiliation. They had played him for an absolute fool. Once he killed Black Pops, the door would be open for Chandler to walk through and take the throne. Tanasha would legitimize him in the eyes of those loyal to Pops - all the blame would fall on Red.

"Muthafucking bitches," Red uttered under his breath. Black Pops noted the moment of realization on Red's face and offered him one of his classic smiles.

"You got something you wanna share," he asked, eyeing Red and the gun still in his hand.

"How did Chandler know where to find me?" Began Red, "don't you think it's strange I'm here, but he isn't?"

"Chandler is good money Red," answered Black Pops.

"Then how did he know exactly where to find me?" Insisted Red.

"What the fuck now Red?" Black Pops said. Just then Suga Momma entered the room from a back entrance behind Black Pops. She hurried over to Black Pops and rapidly began whispering in his ear.

"You muthafucking shittin' me baby!" He exclaimed. Red and Tammy stood in alarm as Suga Momma placed her hands on her hips nodding her head up and down.

"Somebody done blew up Big Ross's crib uptown. They say everybody's dead!" Black Pops sounded both pleased and mystified by the news. Red and Tammy looked at one another. He could see fear in his sister's eyes.

"Did you know Tanasha..." Red began, then stopped. Black Pops looked him up and down.

"What about her?" He asked, his mirth cut short.

"I think she told Chandler where to find me. But I don't think Chandler let you know that. If my guess is right, these niggas been following me since this afternoon."

"You saying Chandler knew where you were this whole time?" Black Pops quizzed skeptically.

"Yes sir," said Red.

"What you saying Red?" Asked Suga Momma.

Chandler and Tanasha are playing us against each other!" He answered.

"Slow it down nigga," Black Pops ordered. "My baby girl can be a trifling bitch sometimes but she ain't no dirty bitch!"

"I feel you Pops, but she looking a little grimy right about now," said Red. Black Pops was on his feet again, smashing a clenched fist down on the desk.

"Now you going to muthafucking far Red!" He yelled. "Suggesting my baby got something to do with all this shit! You ungrateful muthafucka you! Get the fuck out! Boy, get the fuck outta here before I take yo nuts my goddamn self!"

"A'ight! I'm out Pops, but I'm gon' prove it before the night is over," Red said, placing the Glock in the back waistband of his slacks.

"You stay away from my muthafucking daughter too. I'll get to the bottom of this shit. Until then..." Black Pops thought for a moment. "You get yo ass up to the Northern Tip and wait there until you hear from me. Now get out!"

Red looked at Tammy then back at Pops and Suga. He took his leave after giving his sister a kiss on the cheek, but not before warning Pops again about Chandler and Tanasha.

Once Red was out of the room, Black Pops let loose a loud, long drawn-out, "FUCK!!!"

Tammy cautiously moved back over to the desk and was forming words to speak when Black Pops looked her directly in the eyes and said, "You know he done fucked up now. Don't no nigga pull heat on me and survive it. You know that don't you?"

"I know daddy, but...but somebody's playing him and you against each other. Please, you gotta forgive him daddy; he's all I got." Tears fell from her eyes which were heavy with mascara.

"What the fuck more you want?" He yelled. "I already gave the nigga a head start!" Black Pops was adamant, Red had to die.

Chapter 12

"Where the hell have you been?" Tanasha froze at the sound of Chandler's voice as she entered her Soho hideaway. In order to contain her growing anger, she had to take a quick, deep breath.

"I was taking care of some business. But I'm here now. Why you sitting up in here in the dark and shit?" Tanasha's heels clicked loudly against the floor as she walked in and set her alligator tote down on the statement white leather couch. She leaned down and kissed Chandler on the forehead then sat down next to him. They both stared out at the panoramic view of the city, shining like a star under the night sky.

"Red showed up at Lincoln Center," he said. "I armed him. Apparently, your father is still alive, which leads me to conclude I'm a wanted man."

"How can you be so sure Red didn't pull the trigger," asked Tanasha as she stroked his back.

"Because Pops been blowing up my phone for the last twenty minutes. It's not like him; so Red must have pussied out and snitched."

"We should have pushed him further," said Tanasha softly kissing his profile. "But the night is still young. He's probably on his way back here now."

Chandler turned and pulled her into his arms. He pushed his tongue into her mouth, she placed her hand in his lap, and began undoing his zipper.
"He's probably figured out you and I are working together." She reached into his pants, pulled out his stiffening dick, and continued to stroke it as they kissed.

"Sit on that big dick momma," Chandler uttered breathlessly. Tanasha gave an inner eye roll, stood up pulling her panties off from beneath her black miniskirt, and then hiked the skirt up around her waist.

Chandler loved the sight of Tanasha's pussy. He loved how she kept it smooth with a tiny little triangle of hair. His dick eagerly jerked in anticipation of her riding him.

"Wait!" Tanasha said. "Suck my clit," and proceeded to balance her foot on his thigh. Chandler didn't hesitate to dive in and begin sucking and pulling on her pussy lips like a starved man. Tanasha moaned in pleasure, thrusting her hips forward meeting his darting tongue.

She grabbed his head and imagined breaking his neck
right then and there, but no. She still needed him alive.
Besides, removing his body from her place would pose
an inconvenient problem with the tenant board.

She slithered her body down until the head of his
ten inch dick entered her then slowly bounced her way
down its shaft like a dancer on a pole. Chandler threw his
head back in ecstasy, grabbed her ass cheeks, and began
pumping in and out while she slathered his neck with
saliva.

Red stood across the street from Tanasha's
building looking up at the top floor. He saw the lights
come on just as he arrived and realized he had just
missed her arrival. Therefore, he knew she was there.
Getting inside the condo undetected would create a
problem though.
Hence, he decided to wait her out. He figured she had her
hands mixed up in so much shit it wouldn't be long
before she re-emerged.

Chandler crouched low behind Tanasha, hitting
her in quick successive strokes as she wildly bounced up
and down on his piece.

He delivered several slaps to both ass cheeks, and like a mantra chanted, "Gimme that good pussy! Gimme me that good pussy!"

Tanasha buried her face in the couch and imagined it was Lil Reggie back there getting her cut. *"Cum soon"* she thought, as she turned her head around just enough so that they locked eyes. She made hers catlike, and hissed, "Get that pussy baby! Put that white on my ass!"

Chandler covered his eyes, moaned, shuddered, and shook as Tanasha began squeezing nut out of him. His dick popped out of her, spraying several tiny droplets of watery cum on her ass cheeks. She looked up at Chandler with veiled disgust then stood.

"Damn T, why you do me like that?" He asked. "You know when you start talking like that and making them eyes I can't hold back."

"Nigga, we got business to handle. We can't be up in here fucking all night. Besides, I'm sure Red will be showing up trying to kick the door down at any minute!"

"Yeah, just like you was sure Red would kill Pops if pushed hard enough," Chandler shot back.

"I'm going to take a shower. You coming?" She asked. Chandler looked pissed off and just stood there.

"Nah. I'll wash my dick off in the sink," he said.

"Eww! Why you being such a little bitch nigga?"

"Hey yo!" Chandler cleared the space between them in a single step and got up in her face. "I'm not Red Tanasha. You watch how the fuck you talk to me! I don't talk down to you; don't play me like I'm some little petty nigga peddling dime sacs."

"Sorry, ok," Tanasha expressed regret, backing down. "Can we go and shower now?"

"Yeah, let's do that," Chandler said with his face still screwed up.

Twenty minutes later, Tanasha's Black Tesla pulled out of her building's underground garage. Red was about to run up on her when he noticed Chandler leaving the front entrance. Bingo! Chandler was oblivious to the eyes on him as he walked a block down to his parked, matte black 2014 Charger. Red rushed him just as he unlocked the door, placing the Glock to the back of his head.

"Tanasha said you'd probably come sniffing back around here." Chandler appeared to be completely at ease as he lowered his hands and arms, flattening them to his sides.

"Thought you was leaving town tonight," said Red. "Taking her with you?"

"I decided to stick around for a little while longer - update my resume first," retorted Chandler. Red slapped him hard across the back of the head with the Glock.

"You got a smart mouth nigga, always got something to say. Like this morning," he said. "Where the fuck she going?"

"To the Outhouse. Pops called her and told her to meet him there. Want a ride?" Chandler said with a snide smirk.

"What you think this is a game nigga?" said Red, pressing the Glock firmer against the back of Chandler's skull. "Get in the car and put your hands on the dash," he added.

Chandler did as he was told, sat in the driver's seat and placed his hands on the dashboard. Red backed around to the passenger side and got in, never taking his aim off Chandler.

"Drive!" Red demanded. Chandler started the car and pulled away from the curb.

"Answers nigga!" Red pushed the butt of the gun against his tempo. "What's good with you and Tanasha?"

"You think I'm gon' tell you our plans just because you got a gun to my head? Come on Red. You know me better than that."

"You know me too," Red countered.

"I do," said Chandler. "You a hot-headed nigga with very little self control...easily manipulated."

"See that's where you wrong nigga," Red contested. "If that was the case, yo ass would already be laid out in a puddle of blood. You will tell me exactly what I wanna know though."

"Do you even know what you wanna know Red?" Chandler turned the ride onto East Houston Street, heading in the direction of Alphabet City.

"How long you been fucking Tanasha?" Red queried.

"Not as long as you," Chandler jeered. "But then we fuck her for different reasons don't we. See you fuck her out of habit just because she was the first bitch to give you some pussy. On the other hand, I fuck her because she is handing me the keys to Pops' empire."

"You a dumb nigga if you think it's gon' be that easy," spat Red. "You think you can run Killa Cartel?"

"Naw. We're dissolving Killa Cartel for a more lucrative venture," Chandler enlightened him.

"New Crop!" Red said with disgust. "Heron, coke, meth, and salvia blend nigga!"

"It pays the bills," said Chandler. "If you weren't so damn idealistic we would have put you on too. But yo ass think you a modern day Robin Hood."

"Yo, you snitched me and Heiress out. That was some coward ass shit nigga!"

Chandler snorted and laughed keeping his eyes on the road.

"You saying it wasn't you?" Red inquired.

"I needed you alive for tonight. I've had Tanasha putting shit in yo head for months now. All for tonight, and you failed. All you had to do was pop that nigga's cap…twist his wig…body his ass…"

"Shut the fuck up!" Yelled Red then fisted the gun against the side of Chandler's skull, this time drawing blood. Chandler laughed hysterically. Red was about to hit him again when he felt his phone vibrating inside his tuxedo jacket. He retrieved it with his free hand and placed it to his ear. Kat's voice wafted into his ear.

"Yo, ya girl bounced. She ran out when I was taking a client back up top," her voice was distorted with music blaring in the background.

"Ok, when?" He asked, never taking his eyes off Chandler, but cursing fate.

"A'ight, good looking. Holla at me if you hear anything new." Hanging up, he immediately dialed Aleide's number, but it went straight to voicemail.

"Should I drop you off?" Chandler laughed.

"Naw, it's all good," Red said. "We just need to make a detour. Pull over."

"I don't know if you know this Red," said Chandler. "But I kinda have to follow Tanasha to the Outhouse. Seeing how you didn't kill Pops as planned, I have to clean up your mess and do it myself."

"This nigga's out of his fucking mind," Red thought in disbelief, threatening to hit him again which Chandler seemed to want no part of. He knew he could only push Red so far before he actually killed him; he had known Red for several years now. Trained with him, and at times was like an annoying, but caring older brother to him. He knew Red had a weakness that more than likely went unnoticed by others - kindness and loyalty.

He figured that would allow him to survive just long enough to turn the tables on Red as he always did whenever Red attempted to best him in chess.

Chandler pulled the car over. They both got out at the same time. Red hurried around to the driver's side and popped the trunk.

"Inside," he kept the Glock trained on Chandler. "Don't underestimate me Chandler," he threatened. Chandler considered engaging him; after all, they were in an open space. He had certainly taken on a gun-wielding adversary before. Ultimately, he thought better of it. Thus far, Red had proven to be too unpredictable.

Tanasha would have to stall for time until he figured a way out. With Chandler secure in the trunk, Red turned the whip around then headed for the FDR Drive going uptown.

Aleide's night wasn't getting any better. After escaping the Northern Tip, she hailed a cab home only to discover she was without funds. She had left her bag and phone at Red's apartment. Upon arriving home, it took her several minutes to convince the cab driver she would be right back out with his money, to which he pulled off in a violent screech calling her a "cheap whore." After all, she was wearing a sheer, lacy tube top and a mini skirt that was more of a decorative men's cummerbund.

Her mother accosted her the second she walked through the door, crying like a mad woman.

"Where have you been!? Where have you been!?" She cried. "Lu Lu is here and making trouble, saying all kinda crazy..."

Just then, a thin, five foot eleven, elf-faced man with slicked back hair, and inky goatee stepped into the hallway of the small apartment.

"What the fuck are you wearing?" He demanded of Aleide. How she had kept him and Red from crossing paths the last two years she would never know. The task was certainly taxing at times.

"Why are you here Lu Lu?" Aleide asked, walking down the short hall that led to a living room with plastic covered furniture centered around a large floor model television, the old school type that still had channel knobs.

"Why am I here!?" He yelled at the top of his lungs. "Because three hours ago, I get a call from one of my boys saying my little sister is running around with some mutt muthafucka lighting niggas up! So you tell me why the fuck I'm here!"

He backed Aleide up against a faux wood paneled wall. She could smell liquor on his breath but he wasn't drunk. Basically, he was always a belligerent asshole.

"Who the fuck is this nigga yo? What he got you mixed up in? He got you selling pussy?" He growled, all up in her face, then turning to their weeping mother. "Look how he got her dressed mama; she selling off her pussy now!"

135

"That's not true Lu Lu! Shut up! You don't know what you're talking about!" Aleide screamed and pushed him off her, but he was quick to grab her wrist and slam her back against the wall.

"No, no Lu Lu," her mother cried in broken English. He ignored her as he always did when he was pissed.

"Who is he?" He demanded. "It's a fucking crime scene over there! It's only a matter of time before swat comes kicking the door in!"

The thought shook Aleide to her core. What if he was right? If his boys had seen her, countless witnesses could have captured them on their phones. NYPD may already have her face!

She panicked! And pushed Lu Lu off of her, giving her just enough room to rush him and slam her foot into his balls. Lu Lu let out a howl that would've changed a crescent moon to full.
He grabbed Aleide by the hair, pulling her down to the floor with him. He caught her across the face with an open palm. She cuffed him across the mouth several times with her elbow until she drew blood.

136

All the while, their mother screamed in the background like a mad woman walking across hot coals.

Aleide sprang up, delivering several kicks to her brother's abdomen. After a moment, she backed away from his balled up figure. *"Red taught me that,"* she thought of all the times they'd play fight, and how sometimes he would grow serious about her knowing how to protect herself. *"Not Jamarcus but Red. It was him the entire time."*

She realized in that moment what it was that drew her to him, yet broke her heart. He was two different people, but she loved them both.

"I'm calling the police Lu Lu; you don't hit your sister!" Cried their mother.

"I'm just trying to talk to her ma; why you buggin'!" Lu Lu said as he slowly climbed back to his feet.

"If you want to know who he is so bad, put your hands on me again," Aleide threatened coming to her mother's side.

"Yo, you tell that nigga he a dead muthafucka yo. And you a dumb bitch for fucking with him!"

"Get out of here Lu Lu," their mother ordered still crying.

"He ain't done nothing to you," said Aleide.

"Yes he has!" Lu Lu screamed. "Look at you!" He said, then stomped out of the apartment with blood in his eyes.

"Momma...we've got to get out of here," warned Aleide. She watched from their third floor window as her brother disappeared down the block.
She noticed the black Charger with the tinted windows pulling up outside her building and began to pace in earnest. Her poor, confused mother was sixty-five and continuously fatigued. Her plum colored house gown and frazzled white hair made her look like a forgetful wizard as she watched her daughter collect a bag and begin filling it with whatever was lying nearest her.

"What you doing Aleide? You no drugs girl, no?

"No momma, we just have to go." Aleide sobbed, snot ran from her nose and mingled with her tears. Her heart stopped when there was a knock at the front door.

"Oh god," she whispered softly. Her mother looked afraid also.

"Aleide," said Red. "Aleide it's me." Aleide flew to the door, leaving a trail of tears behind her and flung it open. She threw herself into Red's arms and buried her face in his chest, wetting the tuxedo lapels.

"I'm so sorry baby to get you mixed up in all this, but I'm here to make it right," he said and kissed her. Aleide pulled away. Red noticed the red welt on her face. They both stepped inside as he shut the door behind him.

"Yo, who hit you? What the..." Red began but Aleide put a finger to his lips.

"Doesn't matter. We have to go," she said. "You have to get me and my mother somewhere safe. My brother's friends saw what happened on Broadway. No telling who else did."

"That's why I'm here." He produced a plastic key card from his tux and handed it to her.

"This unlocks a locker in Penn Station. Inside is some money, enough to get you far enough away from here for the time being. I want you and your moms to get in a cab, go down there now, and wait for me."

"What! No, no you aren't going anywhere!" Aleide cried.

139

"Listen Aleide. This is some real life and death shit here, ok." Red warned, taking both her hands into his. "Grab a few things for the both of you and clear the fuck out of here. Lose yourself in the crowd at Penn Station. Have some coffee and a donut, and wait for me."

"Aleide, Marcos," said her mother clutching the wall with one hand, her heart with the other. "What is this here?"

"Um...Mrs. Dos Santos…"

"No let me," Aleide interrupted. "Momma. Alguns homens maus estão chegando e nós temos que sair agora. Caso contrário, eles vão nos matar." *("Momma. Some bad men are coming and we have to leave now. Otherwise, they will kill us.")*

O que Marcos fez? Ele é um homem bom, sim?" *("What has Marcos done? He is a good man yes?)* Fresh tears fell from the old woman's eyes as she focused on Red.

"Please come with me momma," cried Aleide. "Eu não posso fazer isso sem você. Você consegue entender isso?" *("I can't do this without you. Can you understand that?")*

Several minutes later, Aleide, now dressed in jeans and long sleeves, stood in front of a black livery cab. After her mother was seated, she returned to Red's and hugged him closely.

"I don't know if we can fix this or not," she whispered in his ear, "but damn you Jamarcus if you don't come back to me, because I love you," she wept.

"Listen, if for some reason I can't, you gotta take that loot and bounce. Take your moms back to Brazil. It should be more than enough to get you set up."

"Don't talk like that," Aleide cried. "Just come back to me," she said, then got into the black sedan next to her grieving mother.

Red's phone rang as the sedan pulled away from the curb. It was Tanasha crying a fit.

"Oh Red baby I was so worried; I haven't heard from you!"

"I'm good ma, calm down. Why you crying like that?"

"It's my daddy Red. He done lost his mind and put a contract out on you. He says he gon' kill you Red." She broke down into uncontrollable sobbing, but Red wasn't falling for any of it.

"He got me on lockdown at the Outhouse; I don't know how long it might be before the nigga wants to kill me too. I need you here baby, please come and get me up out this bitch. I think he already killed Heiress. I heard her screaming like they were interrogating her..."

"Heiress!" Red bellowed.

"They already had her when I got here. My daddy says she was working with Lil Reggie and shit, but I know he's lying."

Red's heart started beating faster. He did aim a firearm at his benefactor, a benefactor who dealt in death, especially to those perceived as lacking loyalty. Consequently, the prospect of a contract on his head was believable enough. He had a mind to leave and join Aleide and her mother now, but he couldn't leave Heiress hanging.

"I'm on my way with Chandler," said Red. "We'll be there in half an hour." He waited for her reaction, but Tanasha had fallen deathly silent.

"You there?" He asked.

"I'll be waiting for you baby," Tanasha answered after several strained seconds of silence.

Red opened the charger's trunk. Chandler lay inside on his back as though waiting for a connecting train.

"Looks like we're going to the Outhouse after all. Tanasha says Pops put out a hit on me, that he's captured and probably killed Heiress, and she might be next on his list.

Somebody's lying," Red acknowledged, "but I don't really give a fuck. I'm done with this shit after tonight."

"There's nowhere you can go where we can't find you Red," Chandler threatened.

"Oh, don't get it twisted nigga," Red responded. "Tonight, you a dead muthafucka. You won't be seeing tomorrow."

Chandler affected a yawn. "I could say the same for you," he smiled. Red snorted hard, spit in his face, and then slammed the trunk down. He looked back in the direction the livery cab had taken Aleide and thought, *"I'll be there."*

Chapter 13

"This shit wouldn't even be going down like this if your dumb ass hadn't called Piper's faggot ass," hissed Tanasha after she ended the call with Red.

"I'm sorry baby, I just wanted to shut that nigga down. He too much trouble baby girl," Suga Momma pleaded apologetically. She attempted to hug Tanasha but her efforts were rebuffed.

"Damn Suga, let a bitch breathe!" She pushed pass the older woman who was still in her couture finery from the evening's earlier event at Lincoln Center.

"Don't worry baby girl, we'll find that nigga! I already put one hole in him; he's bleeding out as we speak. We'll get what we need from him when we catch him then finish the job." She reached out and lovingly stroked Tanasha's hair.

"You should have made sure his ass never made it back here in the first place!" Screamed Tanasha, slapping Suga's hand away. "You had the key code to the niggas safe for the past two days and didn't say shit.

And when you did get the chance to cap his ass, you missed the kill shot and only grazed him. So don't give me that you gon' finish the job shit!"

Tears filled Suga Momma's eyes. "I would've done it at the Mayor's Ball baby, but he was surrounded by Tammy and her bitches after we got word on what happened uptown with Ross's peoples. We needed him alive anyway. Even with the combination, we can't open the safe without his thumb print. But I promise baby, once we find that nigga..."

"What is it!" Tanasha held up a finger to silence Suga Momma and massaged a small Bluetooth ear bud in her left ear.

"We got some activity going on down here." It was Ivy's static-laced voice. Tanasha grimaced, "what kind of activity?"

"I got two niggas down - single shots, probably from a distance. It don't look like Pops' work," he advised.

"Heiress," said Tanasha bitterly. "Look like the bitch really is here. Be careful and keep me posted," she said.

"Ok, I got you," Ivy signed off.

"I lied to Red about Heiress to get him to come down here and the bitch really shows up!" Tanasha cursed. She dialed a number on her phone and listened to it ring several times before Lil Reggie picked up.

"What's good ma?" Was all he said.

"Did you get yourself patched up yet?" She asked impatiently.

"Yeah, I'm chillin' ma. Me and my niggas heading yo way right now. You find yo pops yet?"

"No. He still hiding somewhere in here with his punk ass. But don't worry, my niggas got the shit locked down. He can't get out without exposing himself. Plus, Suga Momma clipped him with her non-shooting ass, so he's bleeding. We got another problem though. My bitch Heiress may be on the premises putting niggas to rest; I could use the extra back up."

"It's all good," said Lil Reggie. "We about ten minutes out. What about yo nigga Chandler?"

"He is on his way back here with Red," she replied. "I don't know if them niggas are working together or not, but I would like them both dead before the night is over."

"Damn, my bitch a muthafucking black widow for real!" Lil Reggie laughed.

"Just get here baby...I'm scared," she cooed then ended the call.

She told Suga Momma, "Backup is on the way."

"What backup is that?" Suga Momma was confused.

Red parked the Charger on the east river side of the sprawling complex of abandoned warehouses that hid Black Pops Outhouse, and forced Chandler from the trunk. The two stealthily made their way to the large, dilapidated construction of rotted metal but discovered all entrances were under heavy guard.

"What's with the welcoming party?" Red asked.

"I don't know," answered Chandler. "Something must be going down, but..." He stopped speaking.

"What!" Red pressed the gun against Chandler's head causing several flakes of dried blood to crack and fall. Chandler gritted his teeth hard. In spite of his tough exterior, he was in severe pain from the two head shots Red had given him earlier.

"The niggas on guard are loyal to me," he said and smiled. "Pops must be dead."

"Tanasha said he was down here running shit and had her on lock. She also claimed he hemmed up Heiress," Red advised. Why you think I even came down here?"

Just then, three SUVs pulled up in rapid succession. A nigga leaned out the window of the lead car and opened fire on the three niggas guarding the door.

"5-0?" Asked Red.

"No way! NYPD some corrupt muthafuckas but they don't do drive by's," Chandler stated.

"Then who?" Red inquired.

"Lil Reggie," said Chandler. "What's he doing here? T was supposed to kill him along with his moms."

"Was she now?" Red snorted a laugh. As he watched Lil Reggie, one arm in a sling, limp into the warehouse followed by approximately twenty men. Chandler felt a tightening in his chest. Tanasha was supposed to meet Lil Reggie with an offer to unite then kill him and Ms. Shirley. She had assured him Lil Reggie was dead; she had betrayed him as well. Red could see what was going on from Chandler's sour expression and laughed.

"Played you too, huh?" He prodded. Chandler remained silent. However, his face said it all. "I'm going in to get Heiress," Red informed him.
"I'll leave you to figure out what to do with Tanasha; I'm done with the bitch and her games." He vacated their hiding spot, leaving Chandler weaponless and alone. Red ran up to the Outhouse entrance and immediately engaged the two men left to guard the door. He unleashed his razor from his wrist and felt the warm spray of blood cover his face, and hands as he opened one of the men's necks.

At the sight of a blood-soaked Red, the remaining guard stepped back in horror, turned tail, and ran.

Red was quick on his heels, jumped him from behind, wrapping his arm around the man's neck and cutting into his jugular, which burst like a water balloon. He heard a clicking sound at his back and turned to find Chandler aiming the first downed man's discarded 9 millimeter in his direction.
He tossed Red the Glock 23 he had dropped, warned him to watch his back, and disappeared. Red caught the weapon and ran toward the sound of gunfire.

149

Mig

"Red!" Red heard his name and immediately detoured toward the familiar voice. He found Black Pops hidden in a pile of rusting scrap metal near the far end of the giant warehouse's first level. Black Pops was soaked in sweat and bleeding from a small wound in his side.

"What the fuck happened to you?" Red asked as he knelt down to help the man to his feet.

"Suga!" Pops answered. That bitch shot me when we got here. Her and Baby girl, my baby girl, are plotting to unseat me. Them niggas tried to assassinate me Red."

"You're a popular man," Red quipped. Black Pops gave him a weak slap to the side of the head.

"I see you got jokes nigga; you come here to finish the job?"

"No, I came for Heiress. Tanasha called me and said you captured Heiress and had her on lockdown. I see she was full of shit now. Her and Chandler been on the up and up against you. Obviously, she done flipped on his ass too and is working with Lil Reggie."

"I'll be goddamned," said a shocked Black Pops.

"But seeing you don't have Heiress, there's no point in me sticking around to add to the body count. I'm out," he announced.

"Nigga, you can't leave me here with these crazy bitches!" Pops pleaded weakly clutching Red's shoulder. Red frowned and felt up the man's side. The bullet had gone completely through.

Regrettably, he had lost a lot of blood. Red's sense of loyalty gnawed at the perimeter of his mind. Then he thought of Aleide and her mother. He was responsible for them now.

"I'm not parked too far from here," he said. "I'll get you to Tammy's and you don't try to find me afterwards."

"Let's go," said Black Pops leaning on Red for support. The two began to make their way to the front entrance when a hail of bullets rained down on them. Red felt the instant, searing burn of being hit in the arm and leg. Nevertheless, adrenaline pushed him to pull Pops along with him toward the back of the warehouse where they took cover in a freight elevator.

Three of Lil Reggie's men came out of the cut and began forcing the door open when they heard the gears begin to move.

"We got Black Pops and some Red muthafucka coming up in the freight," one of the men talked into a smart watch on his wrist. "I don't know which floo..." Unfortunately, he wasn't afforded the opportunity to complete his sentence as Heiress sprayed him and his colleagues with bullets.

Chandler reached the boardroom to find Tanasha, Lil Reggie, and Suga Momma rushing from its crested doors surrounded by several men. He slipped into a storage closet and held tight.

"Them niggas are headed up," Tanasha was saying as they passed him. "See if you can force them out onto the roof!"

"Fucking bitch," Chandler cursed under his breath. He crept from his hiding space and tailed them up a flight of stairs which led from the basement where they were, up to the first level.

Red and Black Pops exited the elevator on the third level of the warehouse and were immediately met by gunfire. He wasn't certain if it was Lil Reggie's men or traitors to Pops. Therefore, he returned fire indiscriminately.

He was in pain from his wounds, but the heat of the moment dulled it down. However, he knew he could only hold them off for so long. With Black Pops' injury, he only had his own prowess to rely on.

He and Black Pops made a run from the elevator to a stairwell to the to their right and headed upwards. "If we can get to the roof, we can cross over to building three!"
He shouted back to Black Pops, dragging the ailing man along with him. Black Pops offered no protest and followed suit. Upon reaching the roof, the two stopped to catch their breath. The cool night air was a welcome reprieve from the stifled air of gun smoke from which they had just escaped. But their rest period was short-lived.

Less than a minute later, Tanasha, Lil Reggie, and a bevy of henchmen burst through the same door and were right behind them. Red and Black Pops hobbled/ran down the length of the roof until they reached its edge. Neither of them was in any condition to make the eight foot jump to the next warehouse's roof. Red looked back to see Tanasha and her new crew laughing, and slowly approaching.

They knew he was out of ammunition, and the blood trail he left was evidence of his wounded nature.

Pop! Pop! Plap! Everyone hit the ground as Chandler rode up behind Tanasha and her crew and began opening fire. Red used the distraction, grabbed Pops, and issued him a quick apology.

Next, he tossed his wounded mentor over the side of the warehouse into the waiting East River below. He looked up to see Tanasha, Lil Reggie, and two other men running toward him guns blazing.

Hot slugs ripped into him, his legs, abdomen, arms, and shoulders. He didn't know how many times he was hit, he wanted to scream out but was already going into shock.

Aleide! He could see her face smiling at him in his mind's eye. *Aleide.*

Red buckled and began falling forward when a harsh impact sent him flying backwards from the roof. He tasted his own blood as it filled his mouth as he fell. There was a loud splash of water as his body hit the East River. On the roof above him, Tanasha emptied her clip, repeatedly pulling the trigger long after it had stopped firing.

Lil Reggie put his hand around her waist and pulled her close. Red watched them share a long, passionate kiss through water logged eyes as his body sunk into the depths of cold water. And then he faded into darkness.

Mig

About The Author

Mig was born and raised in Oakland California.
He now lives with his wife and children in New York
City where he works as a graphic artist at emigliarts.com

www.ingramcontent.com/pod-product-compliance
Lightning Source LLC
Chambersburg PA
CBHW071259130626
46556CB00003B/1383